A Small Hill to Die On

ALSO BY ELIZABETH J. DUNCAN

A Killer's Christmas in Wales
A Brush with Death
The Cold Light of Mourning

A Small Hill to Die On

A PENNY BRANNIGAN MYSTERY

Elizabeth J. Duncan

Minotaur Books

A Thomas Dunne Book

New York

A THOMAS DUNNE BOOK FOR MINOTAUR BOOKS.
An imprint of St. Martin's Publishing Group.

www.thomasdunnebooks.com
www.minotaurbooks.com

ISBN 978-1-250-00824-4 (hardcover)
ISBN 978-1-250-01733-8 (e-book)

First Edition: November 2012

10 9 8 7 6 5 4 3 2 1

For my Humber College friends, students, and colleagues

Acknowledgments

*T*hank you to my editor, Toni Plummer, at St. Martin's Press and my literary agent, Dominick Abel.

In Wales, I'm grateful to Eirlys Owen for translation help, Sylvia and Peter Jones for their inspiring photographs and travelogues, and PC Chris Jones of North Wales Police Service for his advice and suggestions served up with nice cups of tea.

In Toronto, Madeleine Matte, Marlene Gaudet, and Carol Putt provided insightful comments that helped shape the manuscript.

I was delighted when author Hannah Dennison offered to read the manuscript. Penny has her to thank for that lovely Italian handbag Victoria brought back from Florence.

And as always, special thanks to my two greatest supporters, son Lucas Walker and our dog Dolly, who inspire me every day.

A Small Hill to Die On

One

*P*enny Brannigan rolled over and glared at the glowing red numbers on her alarm clock. Four o'clock in the bloody morning. She'd done all the right things to prepare for a good night's sleep: a luxurious soak in a warm, fragrant bath, a cup of soothing chamomile tea, and relaxation exercises involving palm trees, turquoise waves, and a pink beach. She'd stretched out between clean sheets freshened with lavender linen spray and opened the most boring book the local librarian could locate—a history of farming practices in the old Soviet Union.

Her efforts had worked, sending her quickly off to sleep. But a few minutes after one o'clock she awoke from an uneasy dream and now, after three sleepless hours shifting around in her bed listening to a BBC radio presenter interview a reality television personality about her new hair extensions, which she liked, and her ex-husband, whom she didn't, Penny was beside herself. Even if I get back to sleep within the next five minutes, she groaned,

I'm going to be a basket case at work tomorrow. Or rather, today. She checked the clock again. Four hours from now. She switched off the radio and stared at the ceiling, allowing her thoughts to go into freefall.

"You look ghastly." Victoria Hopkirk looked up from her computer as Penny slid into the chair in front of her desk just after nine. "Thank you very much," moaned Penny. "I feel awful. I was awake half the night."

"Trouble drifting off?"

"Oh, I drift off all right but I just can't seem to stay asleep. I wake up and can't get off again. Honestly, it's driving me mad. I haven't had a proper night's sleep for weeks. I just lie there listening to rubbish on the radio and thinking about things. Like what happened to that poor woman whose body was found in the old ductwork."

Several months earlier Penny and Victoria had bought a decaying old stone building beautifully and gracefully situated on the bank of the River Conwy and had overseen its conversion into an airy, bright, modern space. But the renovations had not gone smoothly. Workmen had discovered human and animal remains wrapped in a tatty old duvet in the ductwork. The body had been identified as that of Juliette Sanderson, who had worked as a kennel maid at Ty Brith Hall, and the animal remains were those of a cat. The woman had gone missing sometime in the 1960s and how she'd died and why her body had been hidden in the building for so many years remained an unsolved mystery.

"We may never know what happened to her," Victoria replied, "and you certainly shouldn't be losing sleep over her.

Have you been to see the doctor? She could prescribe something."

"No! I don't want any tablets. You never know about side effects with those drugs. They might make me dopey." Victoria raised a well-shaped eyebrow. "Dopier?" emended Penny.

"Well," said Victoria, "I hope you're going to be able to function well enough during the day to manage the Spa on your own because, if you'll recall, I'm taking some time off, starting tomorrow. We both put in a tremendous amount of work getting this place up and running and we deserve a break." She smiled. "It just so happens that I'm taking my break first."

Victoria opened the top drawer of her desk and pulled out a glossy brochure. Holding it in both hands at arm's length, she displayed the cover to Penny.

Penny's eyes swept over a photo of an idyllic farmhouse overlooking a neatly laid out vineyard. The image was bathed in the soft, warm light of late afternoon as wispy clouds drifted through a brilliant blue sky.

"Tuscany? In January? I hope you're not expecting it to look anything like that. No rustic villas and sun-dappled piazzas for you, I'm afraid. It's bound to be every bit as cold and miserable as it is here."

"Well, it may be, but the point is, it's not here. It's there. That's what's so great about getting away. A nice change of scenery always works wonders. And it's the off-season, so I've found a good deal on a *pensione* in Florence." She grinned. "There are some concerts that I'd love to go to and I've signed up for a cookery course with wine tasting. I really just made the decision to go last minute and got a fantastic package deal. I'm so excited."

Penny's face went blank.

"What's the matter?"

Penny held up a finger and gave a loud sneeze.

"Maybe that's your problem. Are you getting a cold?"

"I hope not. That's the last thing I need right now. Anyway, you'd better tell me what I need to know about looking after the business while you're away." Penny cupped her chin in her hands.

A few minutes later a gentle, reflective smile spread across her face as Victoria wrapped up her explanation on how she managed the day-to-day operations.

"Seriously, I hope you have a fantastic time. How long will you be away? A fortnight?"

"Actually," Victoria replied, "I was thinking a bit longer than that. Since I'm going anyway, I was thinking more like a month. Or maybe even six weeks."

As Penny's smile faded and she started to protest, Victoria held up a hand.

"Sorry, Penny, but it's all settled. I'm going. And anyway, it's not like the old days. I'll take my laptop, and if there are any problems or you've got questions, you just have to contact me and I'll get back to you right away. Sorted! There's Wi-Fi everywhere to check e-mail and I'll have my mobile with me. I'll show you everything before I go. How to do the banking and all that. Rhian has a good grasp of the business end of things. You'll be fine, and honestly, I do need to get away."

Penny checked the time, gave the desk a little tap, and stood up. "Right, then. I'd better go. Mrs. Lloyd'll be arriving any minute for her manicure."

"I heard at the Over Sixties Club that we have some interesting newcomers in our midst," Mrs. Lloyd remarked as Penny began removing last week's nail polish. "Vietnamese people, they are, or at least everyone except the husband is. He's English. There's the mother and two teenagers and the mother's brother, and you'll never guess where this lot is living."

Penny set down a scrunched-up cotton ball covered in brown nail polish and lifted the lid from a glass bowl where she kept clean cotton balls. "Where?"

But before Mrs. Lloyd could reply, Rhian, the receptionist, poked her head around the door.

"Penny, could I just have a quick word, please." She gave Mrs. Lloyd an apologetic smile. "Won't take a minute."

Penny and Mrs. Lloyd exchanged quizzical looks and Penny stood up.

"Excuse me. I'd better see what she wants."

"Yes, you better had."

Two

Penny joined Rhian in the hall that led from the manicure room to the reception area of the Llanelen Spa.

"There's a woman in reception demanding to speak with the manager. Victoria's stepped out to pick up some bits and pieces for her holiday, so it's down to you, I'm afraid. You'll have to speak to her. She's quite insistent." Rhian lowered her voice. "She's Chinese, I think." Penny nodded. "Right, I'll talk to her. You go back to work now." The two women walked down the hall, their footsteps making soft, padding noises on the hardwood floor. Rhian settled herself in front of her computer, and after a quick glance at the visitor, she began typing.

An Asian woman standing in the reception area turned to Penny and gave her a cool, professional smile. She was several inches shorter than Penny and wore her black hair tied back in a ponytail. Her small dark eyes darted about, taking in everything.

"Hello," she began. "My name is Mai Grimstead and my

family and I have just moved to Llanelen. I'm opening a new business here and wanted to speak to the manager. Would that be you? Might I know your name? Are you the manager?" She spoke with a British accent that seemed at odds with her appearance. While her accent had the faintest hint of something foreign, most pronounced was the downward intonation at the end of each sentence associated with Birmingham.

"Yes, I'm Penny Brannigan, one of the owners," Penny said. "Is there something I can help you with?"

"No, I don't need any help," the woman replied. "I'm just paying you a courtesy visit, that's all."

"Oh, really? That's very nice of you."

"Yes, you see, I'm going to be opening a new business on Wrexham Street. Where a bookstore used to be, or so I was told." Penny waited, a mild fluttering of apprehension starting up within her. She didn't like what she was hearing and was afraid of what Mai was about to say. Before she could reply, Mrs. Lloyd's head peered round the door of the manicure room, and then the rest of her entered the hallway.

"It's all right, Mrs. Lloyd," Penny reassured her. "There's nothing to worry about. Everything's under control."

"I thought I heard someone mentioning the old bookstore," Mrs. Lloyd said as she approached Penny. Her curiosity had got the better of her, as it always did, and she turned her full attention to the Asian woman.

"The bookstore closed a little while ago, what with everybody buying their books online or reading them on those funny little device things. Shame, really, but if someone's that desperate for something to read, there's the public library, and the charity shop has a perfectly good selection of used paperbacks.

And hardbacks, too, with their jackets still on them. And fairly recent, they are, so I'm told."

"I'm not interested in books," said the woman, turning her attention back to Penny. "My research showed this town doesn't have a tanning facility. But that's about to change."

Mrs. Lloyd cocked her head. "Is it?"

"Yes," said Mai.

"Look, I'm sorry, I haven't explained myself very well. I own a chain of nail bars and tanning salons across the Northwest. We've several locations in England, Chester being the closest, but we're expanding into North Wales. Nailz. Have you heard of us?"

"Oh!" said Mrs. Lloyd, exchanging a concerned glance with Penny. "Yes, of course I've heard of Nailz. And you own it, you say?" She thought for a moment. "And when will you be opening?"

"Soon. The builders have started converting the premises where the old bookstore used to be. And because we just need a few fixtures and fittings, we'll be up and running in no time. The new shop is going to be called Handz and Tanz because we're adding tanning to the services we offer. That's Handz and Tanz with a zed."

She turned to Penny. "So I thought the proper thing to do would be to stop in and tell you myself about our plans. I didn't want you to learn about us from the newspaper." She gave a light, slightly embarrassed laugh. "Or even, possibly, from one of your former clients."

Penny did not immediately reply as she struggled to take in the implications of what she had just heard.

"I'm sure your tanning service will be in great demand," said

Penny sarcastically, with a strong emphasis on the word "tanning." "Of course, studies have shown that tanning is dangerous, so that is not a service we offer as we place an emphasis on health and well-being." Rhian glanced up from her computer. "Now then, if there's nothing else, I'm afraid I'm going to have to ask you to excuse me. I must be getting on. Mrs. Lloyd and I are in the middle of her manicure."

"Yes, well," said Mai, "I just wanted you to know. You'll see the shop sign installed in a day or two. I have to be getting on as well. Lots to do what with launching our newest venture and seeing the family settled into the new house."

Mrs. Lloyd raised an eyebrow and shot Penny a conspiratorial glance.

"Before you go, er, Mrs., when you say 'house'—bought a place in the area, have you?"

"Yes. It's called Ty Brith Hall. Do you know it?"

Penny tried to conceal her surprise.

"We know it," said Penny. "We heard at Christmas that it'd been sold, but we didn't know who had bought it."

"Well," said Mai, pulling on her gloves, "now you do." She gave a curt nod and turned to go. Rhian stood up and the three watched Mai push open the door and step out into the frosty January morning, letting in a whoosh of cold air.

"Well, I don't know what to make of that," said Mrs. Lloyd as she and Penny returned to the manicure room and work resumed on Mrs. Lloyd's fingernails.

"But I do think that woman's going to be trouble with a capital *T* for you, Penny, you mark my words," said Mrs. Lloyd. "A foreigner. We don't get many foreigners moving to Llanelen." She thought about what she had just said and to whom she had said it. "Well, there's you, of course, but that's different. You're from Canada and we used to practically own Canada, back in the days when we still had an empire, so in a way, you're one of us."

Penny had arrived in Llanelen over twenty-five years ago as a recent university graduate with a degree in fine arts. She had planned to stop in Llanelen for just the one night, but as the years slipped away she had created a life for herself in the small market town. She'd made friends, built up a small manicure business, and on the death of a dear friend, a retired schoolteacher with no family, she had inherited a period cottage, which she had lovingly updated and decorated.

The two women fell silent and the only sound was the soft scraping of emery board on fingernail. After a few minutes, as if unable to bear the silence, Mrs. Lloyd picked up where she'd left off.

"What is the world coming to when someone like that would live at Ty Brith Hall? I wonder. The country's being taken over by foreigners. I don't care about political correctness and what we're allowed to think or say. Very worrying, it is," she said. "Those politicians are letting these foreigners come in and steal our country. Everyone's so concerned about not offending anybody we're not allowed to be British anymore." She gave her head a little shake. "And Ty Brith Hall, of all places."

Beautifully situated on a hill overlooking the North Wales valley town of Llanelen, and with embracing views of the magnificent ancient green hills that cradle it, Ty Brith Hall had been owned by the Gruffydd family for decades. Emyr Gruffydd had inherited the property the previous summer on the death of his father, but now spent most of his time managing the family's other estate in Cornwall. Too many unhappy memories attached

11

to the property, the townsfolk suggested. Or too much house and land for a single man to cope with on his own.

"We don't know anything about this woman, really," said Penny. "We're just going on first impressions. I hope we're not being racist. But I must say I found her accent rather surprising. Where's she from, do you think?"

"Birmingham, I shouldn't wonder. We had a woman who worked in the post office once who sounded like that." She gave Penny a meaningful look. "I'm not an expert on accents by any means, but I'd say from the sound of hers she's been in this country a very long time. Grew up here. Maybe her family arrived here with the boat people in the 1970s, so she might even have been born here."

Penny wiped her hands on a towel, looked at it thoughtfully, and then folded it.

"What I don't understand," Mrs. Lloyd continued, "is why on earth Emyr would sell the Hall to her. That house has been in his family for decades and he loved it. Why would he not want it to go to someone who would appreciate it and take care of it? I can't see her doing that. What could she possibly know about or want with country living? It's not for everyone, you know."

"Well, these are difficult times. I don't suppose there are many people about who could afford a property like that, so he probably didn't have much choice who he sold it to." After a moment's reflection, she added, "Of course, entertainers and show business people are always looking for nice big country estates. Wouldn't it have been something if we'd got a film star? Or a couple like Brad and Angelina. They buy up houses all over the place. France . . ."

Mrs. Lloyd reached for a tissue and dabbed at her nose.

"Well, that's another thing. Who knew there was so much money to be made in tanning salons that you could afford a beautiful place like Ty Brith Hall. She must be rolling in it."

Penny sighed as she applied the top coat to Mrs. Lloyd's manicure.

"Actually, right now I don't care about her buying the Hall. It's the new business that's got me very worried. I don't care about the tanning. If young girls or older women who should know better are stupid enough to pay to expose themselves to skin cancer, that's their lookout, but this town doesn't need two manicure salons. Never mind Handz and Tanz with a zed. With a zed! How stupid is that?"

"And you do know, Penny, that these foreigners who run the nail bars will probably charge much less than you do. They'll have brought in those girls who work cheap."

Penny gave her a sharp look as she placed Mrs. Lloyd's hands under the nail dryer. "Oh, I wish you hadn't said that, Mrs. Lloyd. Now you've got me really worried."

Mrs. Lloyd gestured at her handbag. "Just reach around in there and find my mobile, would you? The moment my nails are dry I'll ring Morwyn and let her know about this woman. I expect she'll want to do a story about her opening a new business." Leaving Mrs. Lloyd to think about what she would say to Morwyn, her niece who worked for the local paper, Penny strode down the hall and asked Rhian if Victoria had returned yet. Told she had and was in her office, Penny knocked on the door and then entered. Victoria, who was crossing off an item on a piece of paper on her desk, looked up, and the corners of her mouth started to draw up into a smile but didn't quite make it.

"Now you look really awful," she said. "Even worse than

you did earlier this morning. What is it? Has something happened?"

"We've got competition." As she told Victoria about the new tanning salon and nail bar Victoria slowly sank back into her chair.

"Maybe I'd better stay home. This probably isn't the best time to be going on holiday."

Penny mulled that over for a moment. "No, I think you should go. The nail bar won't be opening for a couple of weeks, so there's not much we can do about it now. Have your holiday. Get rested up and come back in fighting form. We'll figure out what to do when you get back, depending on what's happening."

She stood up.

"We thought we took everything into account in the business plan, but we didn't allow for competitors." She paused. "Or should I say, *competitorz* with a zed?"

Three

Mai drove the last kilometre up the long and winding driveway to Ty Brith Hall. Most people making that trek paused for a moment to admire the far-reaching views that stretched across the fertile valley to the hills beyond, but Mai ignored her surroundings, keeping her eyes focused on the road ahead.

She pulled the car round to the back, got out, and after giving the car door a good slam, she picked her way across the graveled yard. She paused for a moment to look around her, taking in the wintry beauty of the richly designed and intricately laid out gardens glittering with frost, and then pushed the door open. The silver dolphin knocker lifted a little and made a tiny tapping sound as she closed the door behind her and entered the well-worn stone-flagged hallway that led to the kitchen.

"Only me," Mai called out as she entered the kitchen.

She shot a hard, dirty look at the man sitting at the kitchen table, who had not bothered to look up when she entered. He turned a page of the tabloid newspaper spread out in front of him, took a long, practiced drag on his cigarette, and then tapped the ash into a saucer. Placing his finger on a column of type to mark his place, he glanced at Mai, grunted, and then exhaled smoke through his nose. He pushed a greasy clump of brown hair out of his eyes and set the cigarette down in the saucer. The smoke drifted to the ceiling in a swirling purple haze.

"You could at least say hello, you bloody great useless prat," Mai said. "How are the kids? Are they even up yet?"

"Look around," the man replied with a dismissive shrug. "Do you see them anywhere?"

"They might have gone out," Mai said, as she filled the kettle. "Have you had your breakfast?"

"No, I was waiting for you to get back and make it," the man said.

"It's practically noon," Mai said, her voice rising. "Do I have to do everything around here? Isn't it enough that I run the bloody business that provided all this for us?" She waved an arm to take in the large kitchen.

"Nobody asked you to," the man replied. "We were fine as we were. We didn't want to move to this godforsaken place. The pubs are rubbish and there's nothing for the kids to do."

As he spoke, a tall, skinny teenager slunk into the room and sat down opposite the man. The boy waved a hand back and forth in an ostentatious display of dispelling the cigarette smoke.

"Mum, can you tell him not to smoke in the house?"

"Derek, how many times? Don't smoke in the house. It's not good for the kids."

Derek sucked in another lungful of smoke and blew it out through his nose in the general direction of the boy but not quite in his face.

The boy muttered something under his breath and stood up.

"Make us a coffee, Mum, and I'll take it upstairs," he said. "I'm not sitting here with that tosser husband of yours." He walked over to the window and looked out.

"I hate this place. I think I'll take the bus into town later. God, I miss my mates." He accepted the mug of instant coffee Mai was holding out to him, and after sloshing a few drops on the floor, he left the room without looking back.

Mai glanced at the coffee spots on the floor and stepped over them to hand a mug to Derek. "Ta."

"Is that all you can say?" she said, giving his shoulder a rough shake. "Ta? And can't you try to get on better with Tyler? He's just a lad."

"Get off," Derek said, hunching away from her.

"What have you got on for today, besides a trip to the betting shop?" Mai demanded. "Meeting up with that good-for-nothing friend of yours, are you?" He shrugged, folded up his newspaper, stubbed out his cigarette and sat back, arms folded across his chest.

"You know, Mai, I don't think coming here was such a good idea. The kids hate it, there's nothing to do, and you don't seem too sure of it yourself. Tell me again why we're here, and maybe you can convince yourself while you're at it."

"You know why we're here. We're expanding the business

into North Wales, and we were lucky to get this place. This kind of property doesn't come on the market very often. It's beautiful here, and once everybody gets used to it, everything'll be fine."

"Yeah, well, you just keep telling yourself that, love." Derek gave her a wry look and raised his eyebrows. He gave himself a good scratch, pushing down the top of a graying undershirt to reveal the forked tongue of a tattooed snake that wound its way around his torso.

"Well, it's your money." After a moment he corrected himself. "Well, your brother's, more like."

"And I intend to make the most of our life here," Mai went on, as if he hadn't spoken. "Join a few organizations, get involved in country life, that sort of thing." Her face softened as she reached out to touch Derek's hand. "Look, for my sake, just try to get along with folk, will you? I want this to work. And for God's sake, keep your tattoos covered up."

"You? Country pursuits? Give me a break." He yawned and gave himself another scratch. "And what's the matter with my tats, I'd like to know? You used to like them well enough. As I recall, you couldn't get enough of them before we got married." And with that he picked up his mug of coffee and slunk out of the room.

"And we all know what a mistake that was," Mai yelled after him. "And mind you don't spill that coffee. I've enough to do without cleaning up after you." It's too bad that little cleaner or housekeeper or whatever she was hadn't agreed to stay on, Mai thought, even though she'd been offered more money. Mai had heard that towns and villages could be closed and unwelcoming to newcomers, but she wasn't worried about that. She had more than enough money to buy her way into the locals' favour. In a few weeks everyone in town would be scrambling to be her best friend. She'd always admired the posh properties advertised in the genteel magazines, and now she had her chance to live that dream. She'd get a pair of expensive leather-lined Le Chameau wellies and one of those dark green puffy vests that duchesses always wore in *Hello!* magazine when they wanted to show everyone how down-to-earth they were, talking about hens or mucking about in the garden just like regular folk. But all that would have to wait until the business was up and running.

She picked up the tattered *Racing Post* Derek had left on the table and stuffed it into an overflowing rubbish bin under the sink. As she straightened up, a shuffling sound in the hall announced the arrival of her daughter, who was wearing pajama bottoms with a pattern of cupcakes, an old bubble-gum-pink T-shirt with ROCK CHICK spelled out in glittery silver letters, and oversize black-and-white slippers in the shape of panda bears.

"I don't feel so good, Mum," Ashlee Tran said as she lowered herself into the chair Derek had just vacated. She gave a big sniff and supported her head in her hands, her dark hair falling like a silky curtain over chubby fingers.

"What's the matter with you, love?" her mother asked.

"I can't stand the smell of that cigarette smoke. And those fag ends make me feel like I'm going to throw up." She pushed the saucer of cigarette butts away from her.

"Well, get some breakfast down you and you'll feel better. Fancy some eggs and bacon?"

Ashlee turned a pasty, sallow face to her, opened her mouth, and jabbed her index finger in front of it. Mai got the gagging gesture.

"I'll take that as a no. Maybe just some cereal, then," said

Mai. "Something light to settle your stomach." She reached into the cupboard, pulled out a cereal box, and placed it on the counter. As she turned to walk to the fridge, she looked thoughtfully at her daughter. She opened the fridge door and took out a carton of milk and gave it a little shake. "There should be enough there," she said, setting it on the table. As she reached back for the cereal box, her daughter sprang up and raced from the room. A few minutes later Mai heard the sound of a toilet flushing. A rising feeling of dread clawed at her stomach as she lowered herself into a chair and stared at the cereal box.

With everything else that was going on, the last thing she needed was a pregnant nineteen-year-old daughter. "Please don't let her be in the club," she muttered under her breath. A moment later she reassured herself. Ashlee couldn't be. She doesn't have a boyfriend. Mai looked at her daughter, now standing in the door frame. She did seem to have gained a little weight, though. But maybe that was just the result of a little comfort eating after all the upheaval of moving to the new place. Finding a bit of solace in the bottom of a crisp bag. It was hard to tell. Unlike her mother, who was extremely slim, Ashlee had a roll of fat around her abdomen, so a baby bump might be difficult to detect. Mai frowned. No, if anything like that was going on, Ashlee would have told her weeks ago, as soon as she suspected. They were so close. Her daughter would never keep something like that from her.

"Ashlee, you'd tell me if anything was the matter, wouldn't you? If there was something going on with you that I should know about?"

"Of course I would, Mum. Nothing's the matter. Everything's fine."

The girl sat down. Mai winced as her chair scraped the kitchen floor.

"I'm not hungry. I'll just sit here for a few minutes and then get something in town later, maybe."

Four

As the bus pulled up at the Watling Street stop in the town centre, Mai's seventeen-year-old son, Tyler Tran, pushed his way past a young woman struggling to get off with a folded-up pram in one hand and a toddler in the other. Once on the pavement he seemed unsure which way to go, so he stood where he'd landed, trying to get his bearings, forcing passengers anxious to board the bus to go around him. An elderly man wearing a frayed plaid flat cap seemed about to say something to him, or perhaps make a general comment on the lack of manners in today's youth, but his wife's restraining hand on his arm, accompanied by a look every husband understands, combined with something in Tyler's scowl and general air of aggression, made him think better of it and he climbed on the bus without saying anything.

Tyler watched the bus disappear over the town's famous three-arched bridge on its way to the neighbouring town across the river. As his breath curled into the crisp air, he peered into a shop window, taking in a halfhearted display of dusty plastic fruit, biscuit tins, and jars of jam stacked to form a triangle. At the base someone had placed a few evergreen boughs, now dry and turning brown, and sprinkled them with fake snow. The window was edged with twisted red and green streamers that had begun to fade under a wintry sun. The display, which would have had little appeal for Christmas shoppers a month earlier, now begged to be dismantled. Jamming his hands into the pockets of his anorak as he turned away, Tyler slouched off down the street in the same direction the bus had gone, not sure what he was looking for but confident he'd know it when he found it.

The younger child of Mai Grimstead and her first husband, a Vietnamese immigrant who had been chosen for her by her family, Tyler couldn't believe what he was hearing when his mother had told him the family was moving to North Wales, a place he'd barely heard of. "You're kidding me" had been his first reaction. His second had been, "Well, you can stuff that. I'm not going and you can all just bloody well piss off." But his uncle Tu', head of the family in a traditional, supreme-authority sort of way, could be very persuasive, and despite himself, Tyler had made the move. Now that the relocation was complete, he refused to go to school and spent his days holed up in his room playing endless, aimless video games and the bloodier the better. He missed his old life, despised his stepfather, and ached to return to Birmingham. He was old enough to leave home. He didn't need anyone's permission. A friend had told him he could sleep on his sofa until he got himself sorted.

As he reached the bridge, the sound of rapid footsteps behind him made him turn around. To his amazement, coming toward him was the most beautiful girl he had ever seen. Her dark hair was piled on top of her head, and as she passed him, she gave him a brief smile as she moved slightly to the right while at the same time he took a step back to let her pass. She strode on for a few more metres, checking her mobile as she went, and then opened a small black wrought-iron gate. After closing the gate behind her and quietly slipping the latch into place, she walked up the little path that led to a large grey stone building crouched on the bank of the River Conwy. She pushed the door open and went inside.

THE LLANELEN SPA read the sign on the building.

Well, this was more like it. Now he had a purpose in life. He had to find out who she was. Maybe her mum worked there. Or maybe she was going to the Spa to do whatever ladies do in places like that, but he didn't think so. She didn't look old enough. She looked young, about his age. He reached into his coat pocket and pulled out a wad of scrunched-up banknotes. He bit the inside of his cheek as he straightened out a five-pound note and shoved the rest back in his pocket. A few minutes later he lifted the latch on the little wrought-iron gate and, heart pounding, made his way down the path to the front door of the Spa.

Five

"May I help you?"

The receptionist smiled at the teenage boy with the dark hair and distinctive Asian eyes.

"Hiya. I was just outside and a girl walked past me and I think she dropped this," Tyler said, holding up the five-pound note. "She's young and has black hair, like, and I'm pretty sure she came in here."

The receptionist stood up.

"Oh, that must have been Eirlys, our manicurist. Just wait here and I'll ring her."

"Ta very much."

A few minutes later Eirlys, wearing a puzzled expression, walked down the hall toward him. "Hello? You wanted to see me?"

"Oh, hi," said Tyler. "We almost bumped into each other on the street back there, and after you'd gone, I noticed this on the pavement, so I thought maybe you'd dropped it, and when I saw you come in here, I thought I'd just . . ."

"Well, that's very nice of you, I'm sure," said Eirlys, "but I didn't drop it. It's not mine."

"Oh."

Tyler, who hadn't thought this far into his scenario, was at a loss for words and remained silent while his brain raced to try to think of something to say.

"Anyway, since it doesn't belong to me"—Eirlys shrugged— "I guess it's yours to keep." In the awkward silence, she turned away from him and peered down the hall. "Well, thanks for coming in. I'd better get back to work now."

"I'm Tyler," he blurted out. Rhian, who couldn't help hearing the exchange taking place in front of her, suppressed a smile.

"Right, well, bye then, Tyler," said Eirlys.

"Bye," said Tyler. "See you around."

As the door closed behind him, he let out a frustrated sigh and then hit his head with his fist.

Eirlys exchanged a quick look with Rhian. "What?" Rhian shook her head, and Eirlys returned to the manicure room.

"What was all that about?" asked Penny, who was stacking the towels Eirlys had just folded on a shelf.

"I've got no idea. Just some lad who found a five-pound note on the pavement, thought I'd dropped it, and wanted to return it to me. I don't know what he was on about." She shrugged and then brightened.

"Penny," she said, "I was online last night and I saw this new kind of manicure and pedicure that uses real snakeskin so the customer gets a nail that has a perfect snake pattern on it. It comes in a kit. Do you think we could order in one or two of them?"

Seeing Penny's look of astonished dismay, Eirlys laughed.

"Oh, no, nothing like that. It's just skin the snake has shed naturally, see. It's not like the snake was killed for it or anything like that."

"Oh, that's all right, then," said Penny. "And tell me, who would be wanting such a manicure? And more important, be willing to pay for it."

"Well, young people, of course, and maybe trendy older ones. Not really old, like Mrs. Lloyd, of course, but you know, sort of old. Up to thirty, maybe."

Penny laughed. "Well, I guess to someone who's what, seventeen are you, thirty must seem kind of old, but believe me, it won't when you get there."

"Anyway," said Eirlys, "you were really good about getting in the bright colours of nail polish teenagers like, so I just thought you'd be well up for giving this a try. I'll show you the advertisement so you can place our order. You have to cut the snakeskin to fit the client's nail bed and then you apply it with a special gel. I know we'll be able to sell them. And they're expensive, too. I think the manicure is about seventy-five pounds."

"All right, you show me and we'll order a couple of the kits."

Six

The middle-aged man scanning a computer screen looked up as the bell jangled to announce the arrival of a punter. "Morning, Derek."

Derek mumbled something as he entered the betting shop.

"Put the cigarette out, Derek, please. You know you're not allowed to smoke in here anymore." Derek flicked a half-smoked cigarette out the door and pulled it shut behind him. He longed for the good old days when the air in any bookmaker's in Britain would have been chokingly thick with the blue fug of heavy smoke.

He paused to scan the lists of horses running that day at racecourses throughout the country. Three other men, and one lone woman, sat at tables impassively watching a horse race on a wall-mounted flat-screen television. No one took any notice of the newcomer.

Using the little pen provided, Derek filled out a betting slip and handed it to the man behind the counter. He glanced at it, then entered a few numbers into his computer.

"Five hundred pounds on Brummie Boy to win in the two thirty at Doncaster?"

Derek nodded and handed him a wodge of grubby banknotes. The bookie's lips curled up slightly in distaste.

"Why can't you use a credit card like everybody else, Derek?" he grumbled. "I hate having to handle all this cash and then count it up at the end of the day."

"Are you saying real money's not good enough for you?"

"No, I'm saying no one uses cash anymore."

He counted the money into a drawer, tapped a few computer keys, and then handed Derek a slip of paper.

"Here you go, mate. Good luck."

Derek pocketed the receipt, scratched his chin, and sat down at one of the tables to watch the races. The bookie's eyes followed him and then returned to the computer screen as a younger man emerged from the back room holding out a cup of tea.

"Him again, is it, Glyn? Getting to be one of your regulars, isn't he?"

Glyn nodded and then gestured to where Derek was sitting. "Five hundred pounds he wagered today," he said in a low voice.

He pointed at the computer screen. "To win." He looked at his companion. "I hope his horse breaks its bloody leg."

"Why, what's that horse ever done to you?"

"It's not the horse." Glyn scowled. "It's what his wife's doing. She's only the one starting up the new tanning service right here in town."

"Oh, so this is about your missus, then, is it?"

"Too right it is. She's got a thing about tanning and with that new shop she'll be in there every other day, wasting her time and our money. And with the two kids and the mortgage, we can't afford it. It's all I can do to keep this place going."

"Well, if your wife likes tanning so much," said the assistant, "maybe she should ask Derek's wife for a job. She'll probably be hiring and your wife has experience, so to speak. And maybe your missus could squeeze in a few minutes here and there on the tanning bed when no one's looking. Just to make sure the equipment's in good working order, like." He gestured at the cup he had set down on the counter. "Now drink your tea before it gets cold."

Glyn gave him a calculating look as he reached for the cup. "You know, that's not a bad idea. You might be on to something there. She was a receptionist at the hotel when we got married. I'll have a word with Derek. Cheers, mate." Feeling much better, he took a cheerful slurp of tea.

Derek continued to stare at the screen. His race wouldn't start for a while yet, but he had nothing to do and this was as good a place as any to do it.

Seven

The little turquoise bus wound its way out of Llanelen. Images of trees and sky flashed by, reflected in the mud-spattered windows, but Tyler Tran was too wrapped up in his thoughts to take any notice of the scenery.

He couldn't stop thinking about the girl he'd met in the Spa. He thought the receptionist had mentioned her name, but it was Welsh and he hadn't quite caught it. But he did remember she'd said the girl was the manicurist.

The bus dropped him off near the road that led up to Ty Brith, and as he trudged his way home, he had an idea.

"Ash," he shouted as he entered the kitchen corridor. "Ash, where are you?"

Derek glanced at his watch. He'd hung around the bookmaker's until after the race and then strolled over to the pub to down a consoling pint of best bitter after his horse came in fourth, and now he was waiting for a friend to join him. Finally, the door opened and a tall blond man entered. He paused for a moment as his eyes adjusted to the light, and then after surveying the room, he headed to Derek's table.

"Bruno. How are you, mate? All right?"

The man sat down and gestured at Derek's pint. "I'll have one of those, if you're offering. Just a half, though. Can't stay too long."

A few moments later Derek placed a pint in front of his companion.

"There you go."

Bruno nodded his thanks and took a long pull on the beer. He licked his upper lip and then sat back. "So how are things?"

Derek shook his head.

"Not so good. The kids aren't settling in and Mai's so wrapped up in opening the new business she can't see how bad things are. I've tried talking to her, but she doesn't get it. She's also worried about Ashlee."

Bruno took a smaller sip this time and set his glass down.

"Oh, yeah, and why's that?"

"Thinks she might be up the duff."

Bruno looked around the pub and then turned to Derek.

"Has she said she is?"

"No, Mai's just suspicious."

"Well, there you are, then."

"What's that supposed to mean?"

Bruno shrugged and stood up.

"I'd better get home. The wife'll be wondering where I've got to."

Ashlee Tran sat opposite Penny and held out her hands.

"I'd like something a little different," she said. "I want it to look special. I heard there's a new polish that crackles so it looks like, I don't know, the back of a reptile. It comes in black." She gave Penny an earnest look. "Or maybe dark purple."

Penny knew instantly what she was talking about and was glad that Eirlys had put it on the list of polishes that appeal to girls. "We do have the polish that gives that broken-up, shattered look, but I've got something else that might interest you. In fact, we just got it in and you'd be the first to have it. What do you think of snakeskin?"

Ashlee's eyes lit up as Penny explained the manicure to her and showed her the promotional photographs that came with the kit.

"But it costs more," said Penny. "And it'll take about an hour and a half. I have to cut the bits of snakeskin to fit each one to your nails."

"Bring it on," said Ashlee. "Let's do it."

Penny studied her nails. "You've been wearing artificial nails, I see." Ashlee nodded. "They're murder on your own nails. I don't recommend them. They're also expensive to maintain, and personally, I don't like the look of them."

Ashlee glanced around her, taking in the shelves with neatly stacked towels and rows of nail polish grouped by colour. The pale pinks, popular in summer, led to darker pinks and into bright reds. Bottles of browns and burgundies, the colour choice in winter, stood at the end of the collection.

"So this is your spa, is it?"

"Yes, we just opened at the end of last year," replied Penny.

"But you don't do tanning, do you? My mother was in here a few days ago. She said you haven't got a tanning bed."

"She's right," said Penny, "we don't. I thought that might have been your mother."

Ashlee nodded. "Of course you did. There aren't too many of us around." Penny ignored the remark.

"Seems a bit odd you coming here when your mother owns a nail bar."

"It hasn't opened yet. It won't open for another day or two. It should have been open by now, but, I don't know, there were problems with the plumbing or something. Whatever. I don't pay much attention to her business."

Penny set out the supplies for the manicure and then began shaping Ashlee's fingernails.

"How are you settling in?" Penny asked. "It can be difficult moving to a new place, leaving all your friends behind." Ashlee gave a little nod of acknowledgment, keeping her eyes on her fingernails. "But there can be something wonderfully exciting about a new beginning," Penny continued. "New places to discover, new friends to make."

Ashlee looked at her and shook her head.

"There's nothing to do here," she said. "My brother and I hate it. We wish we'd never left Birmingham. We were happy there. It was home."

"I can understand that," said Penny. "But you have to give the new place a chance. Who knows? Maybe you'll meet a nice boy."

Ashlee's mouth twisted slightly into a pinched, somewhat haughty look.

"Oh, I'm not interested in boys." The emphasis on the word "boys" was light but enough.

An hour and a half later, Ashlee admired her fingernails. "There you are," said Penny. "The girl with the snakeskin manicure." Ashlee gave her a vacant look and then smiled broadly.

"They're brilliant. I love them!"

Penny returned the smile. "I'm glad you like them. And no one else around here has anything like them, as far as I know. They should last two to three weeks. Depends on how fast your nails grow." She touched Ashlee softly on the arm.

"You know, Ashlee, someone gave me a bit of advice many years ago at a time in my life when things weren't going well. He said the best way to make yourself feel better is to help others." Ashlee raised her gaze. "So," continued Penny, "if you've got some time on your hands, you might feel better if you did some volunteer work. Find a cause you'd like to support and give them some of your time."

"Like what?"

"Well, Alwynne Gwilt is always looking for help in her little museum or there's the seniors home. You could be a visitor and read to the residents. The charity shop might need someone. Or the library, if you like books. Volunteering would get you out of the house, and at the end of the day, you'd feel great knowing you've done something to help others."

Ashlee studied her snakeskin nails. "I don't know." She shrugged. "I'll think about it, I guess."

"You do that." Penny handed her a slip of paper. "You can pay Rhian on your way out. Thanks for coming in."

Ashlee took the paper, sighed, and cautiously, as Penny held her coat, slid her arms down the sleeves, protecting the snake-skin nails.

Penny walked her a little way down the hall and said good-bye. She watched as Ashlee stopped at Rhian's desk, where she paid in cash. She then pushed open the door and was gone.

"Well, how did it go?" Tyler had heard Ashlee's car and opened the back door to let her in.

"Let me get in out of this perishing cold, will you?" Ashlee said. She removed her coat and threw it at her brother. "Here, make yourself useful and hang that up." He slung the coat over a hook in the hall and then hurried after her down the corridor into the kitchen. "What's to eat? I'm starving." Ashlee pulled a yogurt out of the fridge and sat down and peeled off the top.

"So, how did it go?" Tyler demanded again. "Your manicure. Come on, tell me."

Ashlee held out her hand and showed him the snakeskin manicure with its shiny pattern of black and silver interlaced diamonds. "Yeah, very cool. But what was she like? What did you talk about?"

"She said I should do some volunteer work."

"What? Why would she say that? What did you say to her?" He thought for a moment. "Did you say anything about me? Did she remember me?"

Ashlee sat back in her chair and looked at her brother.

"Tyler, she's way too old for you. What are you thinking? Have you got some kind of mother complex?"

A snarly look of confusion chased away the eagerness on Tyler's face.

"What are you talking about? Too old?"

"She's older than Mum, for God's sake."

"No!" said Tyler. "She's my age. She's got dark hair and she's Welsh."

"Well, that wasn't the one who did my nails, Tyler. You said to make an appointment with the manicurist and I did. She's got an American accent, her hair's red, and she's well old enough to be your mum." Seeing his bewilderment, Ashlee laughed. "Oh, and you owe me seventy-five quid for the manicure."

Tyler slammed his chair into the table, kicked the counter, and throwing her a scowl over his shoulder that looked like thunder, stormed out.

Ashlee smiled as she admired her nails. She picked up the yogurt container and, as she dipped her spoon into it, twisted the little pot slightly so she could read the label. Butterscotch pear. Her favourite. But as a sudden rising swell of nausea churned its way up from her stomach, she covered her mouth and made it to the downstairs loo just in time.

Eight

The short days of January stretched on into the next week. Some days the sun struggled to break through the clouds, casting a pale, watery light that bathed the grey stone buildings in a gentle glow. Other days were washed out by freezing rain that rattled windowpanes and kept sensible townsfolk indoors. And then came one of those unexpected warm spells that last a day or two, lifting spirits and reminding everyone that spring will indeed return to the valley and that the end of another winter would soon be in sight.

On the second warm day, a Sunday, Penny called her friend Alwynne Gwilt to see if she wanted to go sketching. Some years ago Penny had set up a little group she called the Stretch and Sketch Club and its members rambled about the valley, sketching, photographing, and painting the wildlife, flowers, stone buildings, and magnificent views that were all around them.

"I don't know how many members we can get together at

this late notice," said Alwynne, "but I'd love to go. I haven't been out of the house since yesterday morning." Alwynne's husband had taken up baking when he retired, and the very sight of him in the kitchen, covered in flour and wearing one of his mother's old aprons, was reason enough to drive her into the fresh air.

"Let's keep it simple," said Penny. "Let's just the two of us go."

"Two? Would you not bring Trixxi?"

Penny looked down at the black Labrador dozing at her feet.

"Yes, of course, Trixxi'd love to come."

At the mention of her name Trixxi gave a couple of half-hearted thumps of her tail and lifted a sleepy head. Penny gave her a gentle rub on her chest with a stockinged foot. Trixxi had been staying with her since Christmas when Emyr Gruffydd had left Ty Brith Hall and, because of his travel schedule, had decided not to take her to his new base in Cornwall.

Gwennie, who had worked at the Hall since she was a teenager and adored Trixxi, had chosen not to stay on and work for the new residents. She now worked for Penny and Victoria at the Spa, ensuring that freshly laundered towels and robes were always available, snacks and light meals were prepared for guests in for a day of pampering, and that the place ran with the clean efficiency of a boutique hotel. She lived with her house-proud sister who had decreed that no creature of fur or feather would ever be allowed in her tidy bungalow. So Trixxi's one- or two-night visit with Penny over Christmas turned into a longer stay, and as far as anyone knew, no one was making any efforts to find her a more permanent home.

So after an early lunch, Penny closed the front door behind her and, with Trixxi on her lead, set off for the Spa, where she and Alwynne had agreed to meet up. As she passed the rectory, the door opened and a small brown dog came bounding out. He ran into the churchyard and then, spotting Penny and Trixxi on the pavement, changed course and ran to greet them. He put his paws on Penny's leg and wagged his tail as she bent down to pat him and hold him by the collar. Moments later a middle-aged woman emerged from the rectory with a dog lead in her hand, and seeing her dog was safe with Penny, she walked over to them.

"Oh, Robbie will take off without me," she complained as she bent over to clip the lead on his collar. "He's the silliest dog in all of Wales."

Penny laughed. "He may be, Bronwyn," she said, "but Robbie's probably also the best-loved dog in Wales."

The rector's wife laughed. "He probably is. We don't know what we'd do without him, Thomas and I. He's brought so much joy into our lives." She took in Penny's backpack. "You and Trixxi off on one of your rambles, are you?"

"Going sketching with Alwynne. We're meant to be meeting up at the Spa in a few minutes, so I'd best be off."

Bronwyn nodded and looked up at the blue sky. "Well, you've got a great day for it."

"Mmm," agreed Penny. "It makes such a beautiful change from all that drizzle. I hate those heavy, dark mornings, don't you? I find it so hard to get going." They exchanged a few more pleasantries. Then Penny and Trixxi walked the short distance to the Spa where Alwynne was waiting for them, leaving Bronwyn and Robbie to enjoy the walk they took every Sunday after church.

Warmly dressed in case the weather turned colder but hoping it wouldn't, Penny and Alwynne set off over the town's three-arched stone bridge, passed the tea shop, and turned down a quiet country road that led to a series of small waterfalls. In

December, as Britain experienced the coldest winter in many years, the falls had frozen solid.

"I wonder how that happens," Penny said as they stopped in front of one of the frozen falls that was now beginning to thaw, making a light, steady trickling sound. "One minute it's cascading down the slope and the next minute it's frozen in place."

"Flash frozen, like?" said Alwynne. "I don't know how it happens, but I see what you mean. It must have to be very cold for that to occur because you'd think the running water would prevent it from freezing."

Penny took a few quick steps as Trixxi pulled at the lead, anxious to get on with the walk. "I'm just going to a take few photos of the falls for later," Alwynne called after her, "because it might be thawed soon. I'll catch you up."

Penny and Trixxi walked slowly on up a gentle incline, and a few moments later, slightly out of breath, Alwynne joined them. Penny pointed toward a wooded conservation area known for its wildlife. "How about over there?" Alwynne nodded and the three of them set off. The woodland was surrounded by a waist-high stone fence with large flat stones set on their edges secured on top, giving the fence a jagged, sharp look.

The two women entered the woods through an opening in the fence and walked a few metres to higher ground.

"This looks like a pretty good spot," said Alwynne, glancing around. "We don't need to go any deeper into the woods, but should we go higher up the hill, do you think?"

"No," said Penny, making a sweeping, encompassing gesture at the view in front of her. "This is good. With the fence in the foreground and the snow-covered hills in the back, we can do a nice landscape." She pulled a field sketchbook and light collapsible stool out of her backpack and unfolded it. She reached in her coat pocket for a dog treat and then unclipped Trixxi's lead. "All right, girl, off you go. See what you can find."

Delighted to have her freedom, Trixxi bounded off down the small hill, tail wagging, as Alywynne and Penny set to work.

With a graphite pencil, Penny sketched the view in front of her. Her concentration was broken when, out of the corner of her eye, she saw Trixxi racing back to her. She sketched in a few more lines and smiled at Alwynne as the dog reached her.

"Alwynne, watch this."

Trixxi sat beside Penny and placed her nose under Penny's right elbow and lifted it. She nudged her a few more times and then sat back and let out a sharp bark.

"She does that at home when I'm on the computer, except without the barking. There's something about me on the computer she doesn't like. Sometimes I have to put her out in the hall and shut the door so she can't get at me."

Trixxi gave Penny's arm another nudge, this time stronger and more insistent. Penny looked at her sketch pad and then down into Trixxi's brown eyes. Trixxi took a few steps backward, crouched down in a play bow, and barked again. She took a couple more steps backward and let out a low, throaty noise somewhere between a whine and growl that sent a message Penny didn't understand or recognize. "What is it, Trixxi? What do you want?" Slightly annoyed, she finally gave in and rose from her stool. Trixxi barked excitedly and then turned and ran off for a few steps. She looked over her shoulder to make sure Penny was following her and barked again when Penny took a few steps toward her.

Alywnne pointed at Trixxi with her pencil. "Looks to me as if she wants you to follow her."

Penny gave her a quick nod and set off after Trixxi, who, as soon as she saw Penny coming closer, turned and, breaking into a trot, headed for a large oak tree near the stone fence. As she approached the tree, she veered and ran straight toward the fence, and when she reached it, she began sniffing and pawing at the frozen ground. She gave a couple of shark barks as if urging Penny to hurry.

Under the bare branches of the ancient oak Trixxi reached out with her front paw and scraped at the ground. As Penny approached, she saw that a shallow, dry ditch ran alongside the stone fence and Trixxi was standing in it. She let out a loud bark, looked at Penny with puzzled concern, and then, using both paws, began to dig.

As Trixxi dislodged a loose pile of brittle, frosted brown leaves, a few fell away, exposing a grayish-blue hand, its fingers frozen in a stiff curl. But it was the fingernails, with their snake-skin pattern, that sent a sickening feeling slithering through Penny's gut.

"Good girl," she said when she reached Trixxi, and with one hand she reached down and, grasping Trixxi's collar, pulled her away from her find. With her other hand, she reached into her pocket for her mobile.

Nine

Within ten minutes, flashing blue lights signaled the arrival of the first police car.

"You'll have to keep well back, now, and leave this to us," one of the officers said to Penny as she pointed toward the shallow grave. He turned to his colleague. "The DCI should be here in a few minutes." As he finished speaking, a slow-moving police Land Rover came into view and then stopped near the opening in the fence. A tall man with silver hair got out of the passenger side and a moment later a woman emerged from the driver's side. With a small wave of acknowledgment at Penny, they approached the scene to be briefed by the officer who had been first to arrive.

In what seemed to Penny like a very short space of time, the scene was transformed from a peaceful rural landscape to something straight out of a television crime show.

Officers donned pale blue Tyvek suits and shoe covers and

erected screens around the body. And then white-suited scene-of-crime officers arrived and disappeared behind the screens.

Penny stayed where she was for a few minutes, watching, and then rejoined an anxious Alwynne, who was holding Trixxi on her lead.

After discovering the body, Penny had climbed back to where Alwynne, unaware of what Trixxi had uncovered, was still sketching. "Alwynne," Penny had started to say but found she couldn't speak. Alwynne glanced at her face, and then, startled, jumped up. "Penny, what is it?"

"Trixxi's found a body. I'm pretty sure it's the daughter of that Vietnamese family that just moved to town. I recognized her from her manicure. I gave her that manicure." Penny pointed to the oak tree. "She's down there, in that ditch, under a pile of leaves."

"Well, should we uncover her?" Alwynne asked. "Is there a chance she could still be alive?"

Penny shook her head. "No, she's dead. All I saw was her hand, but it's blue and looks frozen. I couldn't bring myself to touch it to try to check for a pulse. Anyway, it's probably best if we don't disturb the remains any more than Trixxi already has."

Alwynne sat down again. "I don't think I want to go and see."

"No," agreed Penny, "you don't."

After handing Trixxi to Alwynne, Penny had gone back down the hill to await the arrival of the police team, led by Detective Chief Inspector Gareth Davies. She described how she'd found the body and told him that she thought she knew who the victim was. The girl with the snakeskin manicure. The manicure she herself had given the dead girl.

Although there was nothing much to see, the two women watched the police activity from their vantage point higher up the hill. A gazebolike structure had been erected around the body and the scene had been cordoned off. The stone fence provided a natural barrier, and uniformed police officers kept the few curious townsfolk who had turned out to see what was happening on the other side of the road.

Eventually, Davies and the woman police officer he was with climbed the hill and joined them.

"You two should head home now," he said. "There's nothing more for you to do here, and we can get your statements in the morning. It'll be dark soon and it's getting cold."

Davies pointed to a police car.

"PC Jones'll drive you home." He bent down and gave Trixxi a pat. "And you, too."

He squeezed Penny's arm.

"How did she die?" Penny asked.

"Blunt-force trauma the pathologist says it looks like," he replied, "but we'll know more after the postmortem. I can tell you, though, it's not pretty. So I'm not going to ask you to look at the body to see if you can identify it. What you told me about the manicure is enough for us to be going on with. How long ago did you do it, by the way?"

"Let's see. Five or six days. I can't remember if it was Monday or Tuesday. We can check the appointment book now if you need to."

The woman police officer jotted down a few entries in her notebook. "No, we don't have to do that now. It can wait."

Davies reached in his pocket and pulled out a little plastic evidence bag. "When she came for the manicure, was she wearing these?" He handed Penny the bag. She flattened it out so she could see better what it contained. She smoothed down the plastic, revealing a drop earring, a silver hook with a teardrop-shaped purple stone. Alywnne, standing beside Penny, leaned in to look at it.

"No, she wasn't. I don't recognize this."

"Did you take that off the body yourself?" Alwynne asked.

"No, the pathologist removed it."

"Didn't he take both earrings?" Alwynne looked puzzled.

"There was just the one. We'll ask her family about it, then. See if her mother recognizes it."

"Her family?" Penny asked.

"We're on our way there now."

The four of them walked together down the hill, with Trixxi bounding along at their heels, past the place where the body lay under cover of the gazebolike structure.

"I've often wondered," Davies remarked conversationally, "how many bodies would remain undiscovered were it not for 'a local woman walking her dog.'"

Penny and Davies had met the summer before, as he investigated the disappearance and death of a missing bride. Their friendship had deepened and now there was no doubt in his mind that he loved her. But he sensed there was something in her past holding her back emotionally, keeping a precious part of her unavailable to him. He hoped that one day she would love him and trust him enough to open that part of herself to him.

"Ring me later," Penny said, as they reached the police car. Jones opened the door and Trixxi jumped in, settled herself on the backseat and, looking around, panted slightly. She seemed very proud of her afternoon's work. It's not every day a dog does something that attracts so much attention and makes people really sit up and take notice.

Sergeant Bethan Morgan steered the Land Rover onto the wide gravel drive that swept around the front of Ty Brith Hall. A few moments later she switched off the engine, but neither officer made any move to get out. Davies looked at the front door.

"This never gets easier." He turned to her as he opened the car door. "I'll take the lead and you offer support. But remember, we're just preparing them to expect the worse and letting the mother know we're going to have to ask her to make a formal identification. The earring might help."

Bethan nodded and a few moments later they were standing on the front step, each one thinking about what they would say when the door opened. They exchanged a quick, conspiratorial glance as if to make sure they were on the same page just as Bethan knocked. Then, as if at an unspoken signal, both reached into their coat pockets and in unison pulled out their warrant cards and held them up at the same moment that Derek Grimstead opened the door.

Ten

Twenty minutes later the two police officers walked slowly down the front steps. When they reached the last step, Derek closed the door behind them and returned to his wife and stepson in the kitchen.

Mai looked at him, her face an ashen mask of disbelief and fear.

"What do you do," she asked, "when the police come to your door and tell you they have reason to believe that your child has been murdered? How do you get through the first hour, and the hour after that? What are we supposed to do now?"

The three of them looked at one another.

"Well, look, love," said Derek finally. "He said the body they found still had to be positively identified, so we don't know for sure it was her. And she was wearing that earring that you didn't recognize. Maybe it's someone else. Another girl, not our Ashlee."

"Nice try, Derek," said Tyler in a low voice.

Mai ignored Tyler's remark. "Positively identified. And who did they ask to do that? Me. And the policewoman said the body they found had a snakeskin manicure. Do you know any other girl with a snakeskin manicure? The police said the manicure lady told them she did only the one. One. And that was for Ashlee." Her voice was becoming louder. "And why on earth did she get that snakeskin manicure in the first place, I'd like to know." She turned on her husband. "Derek?"

Tyler, who looked shaken, stood up.

"I'm going to my room. I won't want any dinner," he said. A few minutes later the vigorous slamming of the door to his room echoed through the house.

Mai buried her face in her hands as tears, suppressed by shock and disbelief, finally came. At first she wept quietly, but soon her body was racked by loud, gulping sobs. Derek stood behind her, afraid to touch her, afraid not to touch her. "Who would have had it in for her?" she wailed. "Who could have done this? She was only nineteen. She didn't even know anyone here."

"What would you like me to do?" Derek asked as she wiped her eyes with her hands and used her sleeve to mop her dripping nose. "I'd better ring your brother. He'll need to know."

Mai did not reply.

And then Derek did the most useful thing he'd done since they got married. He went off in search of a box of tissues.

Eleven

"Jow did she take it?" Penny asked. With the scene processed and the body dispatched to the morgue, Davis had sent his sergeant, Bethan Morgan, back to Llandudno to begin the paperwork. Instead of ringing Penny once the family had been informed, as he'd promised, he'd driven over to see her.

They were seated on her living room sofa—he holding a glass of beer as Penny sat turned toward him with one leg tucked under her. Between them was a plate of Brie cheese with oat biscuits and sliced apples. He reached for a piece of apple and bit the end off it.

"She was exactly what you'd expect. Disbelief at first. No, it couldn't be her daughter. Shocked, shaken up. Blamed herself. Too busy with the store opening to pay enough attention to her daughter." He shrugged. "The girl was nineteen. It's difficult for a parent to manage their children's lives at that age. You can't control them. Technically she was a teenager, yes, but really more of a young adult." He took another bite of apple, and then a sip of beer.

"There was one thing, though. The mother said she was worried when Ashlee didn't come home last night because she doesn't have a boyfriend and it wasn't like her to stay out. She thought of calling us but decided not to because the police are so bloody useless. We'd just tell her the girl's nineteen, she's old enough to stay out all night if she wants to . . ." His voice trailed off and he sighed. "Unfortunately, she got all that wrong. We would have tried to find her. There are things we could have done."

"Such as?"

"Well, for one thing, we could have tried to find her using her cell phone to pinpoint her whereabouts. We can track signals from the relay towers. Gives a pretty clear idea of where someone is. Or at least, where the phone is."

He set his beer glass down.

"The mother did ask a very intriguing question, though."

"What was that?"

"She asked why someone would want to kill her nineteen-year-old daughter. We're going to need to know the answer to that, too."

He gave Penny an apologetic look and then rested his head against the back of the sofa.

"Sorry to be going on so long about this. You know, I was hoping you and I could get away at Christmas, just the two of us, but then the Harry Saunders case came along, and now I was hoping maybe we could take a few days at St. Dwynwen's Day. Go somewhere nice. Warm, maybe. And now this."

"I couldn't leave anyway," said Penny. "Not with Victoria away. We agreed that one of us would always be at the Spa."

Davies nodded. "Oh, right. I forgot she's away. How's she doing? Enjoying herself, is she?"

"She's fine. She wants to stay on in Florence for another week. She's being very coy about her reasons, but Eirlys thinks she's met a man." Penny took a sip of wine. "Funny that. For one so young, Eirlys can be remarkably perceptive about many things and she might just be right about this. But Victoria hasn't said anything to me about meeting a man, and if something like that was going on, if she's met someone, she'd tell me." She paused. "At least, I think she would."

Davies picked up his glass and took a sip. "I'd like to go back to Ashlee. Tell me about the manicure."

"Right, well, it was Eirlys who suggested we get in the snake-skin manicure kit. When I saw the hand with that manicure, I knew right away it was Ashlee—it had to be."

Davies set his glass down, leaned back, closed his eyes and stifled a yawn.

"Enough for one day?"

He nodded. "But we don't know for sure yet that it is Ashlee," he said in a flat, tired voice. "Her mother will have to identify the body in the morning, and then if it is her, I'll interview the family. We'll start with them. The young lad, the brother, didn't have much of a reaction. He didn't seem too upset, but maybe that's just him being a teenager."

"Neither one of them was happy here, apparently. Ashlee or her brother. They weren't settling in very well. They missed home."

"Where's home?"

"Birmingham."

"Birmingham. Ever been?"

"Yes, of course. I went to a charming little jewelry museum there once."

Davies gave her one of his looks.

"Now you're going to let us handle this, aren't you? There's nothing here that involves you, so there's no need for you to go poking around." He raised his eyebrows at her. "You'll give your statement and then stay out of it. Agreed?"

Penny nodded and rose from the sofa. She started toward the kitchen and then turned around.

"Do you think she was killed there or was she killed someplace else and the body dumped?"

Davies grimaced.

"I knew it wouldn't last."

"Well?"

"The pathologist isn't sure and says he won't know until he's done the postmortem. He'll know more then, but he says it looks as if she was beaten somewhere else and died as she was being moved or she died on that small hill."

Twelve

"Is it my imagination, Penny, or is it just a coincidence that you always seem to be first on the scene when there's been a murder?" Mrs. Lloyd handed her coat to Penny as they walked down the hall toward the manicure room. "Now you must tell me everything. How shocked you must have been to come across a dead body like that. And while you were out on one of your little drawing expeditions, too. Still, I suppose if you hadn't found the body, it might have lain there until spring. I did hear tell of a very haunting story once. The police suspected that someone had been killed but it was winter and the snow was very deep and they couldn't find the body, so in the end they said, well, we'll just wait until spring, and when the snow melts, the body will likely surface.

"Actually, I'm not sure if I heard that or read it somewhere, but it makes you think, doesn't it?"

Penny ushered her client into the manicure room, where

Eirlys was waiting for her. "There you go, Mrs. Lloyd," said Penny. "Eirlys will be taking care of you today."

Penny and Mrs. Lloyd exchanged glances, and Penny shook her head slightly. Mrs. Lloyd understood that there was to be no more talk of the discovery of the body in front of Eirlys.

"Oh, excellent. Eirlys always gets the water temperature just right. You, Penny, tend to make it too hot." Mrs. Lloyd made a coy little gesture and laughed lightly.

"Or maybe that's just me getting old and I can't tolerate hot water the way I used to."

Knowing what was expected of them, Penny and Eirlys both protested. "You? Old? Don't be silly!"

Penny stood for a few moments to chat with Mrs. Lloyd while Eirlys began shaping her nails. "How's Florence?" she asked. Mrs. Lloyd had met Florence Semple a few months earlier and invited her to live with her as a companion and lodger.

"Oh, she was in one of her moods when I left this morning," replied Mrs. Lloyd. "She can be very negative, that one, so I just left her to get on with it." Florence loved cooking, and as the waistbands on her skirts and trousers could attest, Mrs. Lloyd was enjoying all the freshly baked scones and home-cooked meals.

"You know we have our hairdresser in place now," said Penny. "Maybe you should give Florence a gift certificate for a day's pampering at the Spa. She could have a facial and get her hair done with Alberto."

Mrs. Lloyd thought it over. "You know, that might not be a bad idea. But I doubt Florence would go for a whole day—she'd think that a sinful waste of money—but she does need to get her hair cut anyway, so maybe a hairdo and a facial and a manicure might be a nice treat for her." Mrs. Lloyd nodded. "Yes, we'll arrange that for her before I leave today. I think her birthday's somewhere around Eastertime, so that would be a nice gift for her."

"Good," said Penny. "I'm sure she'll enjoy it."

"I just hope she won't think it's all a waste of money," said Mrs. Lloyd. "You know she's never had very much and I think she cuts her own hair." Eirlys looked shocked.

"Eirlys, love, you grew up in a time of plenty. You don't have to worry about money. But women like Florence, who had to scrimp and save just to scrape by, well, life's different for them."

"Yes, Mrs. Lloyd."

"Oh, Penny, speaking of scraping by reminds me. I just heard today that someone who used to live here has apparently moved back to Llanelen. I don't know where she's been all these years, but apparently she's been spotted wandering through some fields outside town looking for ferns or bracken or whatever."

Mrs. Lloyd paused for a moment as Eirlys placed her hands in the warm, fragrant water of a soaking bowl.

"So that got me thinking. This woman, Dilys Hughes her name is, used to make all kinds of lotions and soaps and what have you. Have you thought about creating a line of beauty products for your salon? Oh, what's that called? Private label? Yes, you could have your own line of all-natural beauty products, sourced from fresh, local ingredients, with Llanelen Spa right on the bottle.

"You'd need a fancy label, but that shouldn't be too difficult for you. You could sketch a picture of the spa and include that in the design. Maybe Dilys could even make something up for you. She had a soap made from rose petals that was quite nice, as I re-call. Lathered up a treat, it did. You could see the bits of crushed pink and red petals right in it. And not only that, the rose petals came right from the gardens at Ty Brith Hall."

Eirlys glanced at Penny, unsure what her reaction would be.

"Well, it was very thoughtful of you to think of us, Mrs. Lloyd, but beauty products and cosmetics have a lot of restrictions on them. You can't just sell products someone whipped up at home. They have to meet a lot of standards to guarantee they're safe."

"Yes, I hadn't thought of that," said Mrs. Lloyd "That'll be all those damned EU regulations. We got along just fine when we ran this country for ourselves without those Brussels boffins telling us how to do everything. We did manage to win the war, after all, with precious little help from them. Still, I do see you'd have to be careful. You wouldn't want to sell a skin care product and have the ladies break out in hives and red rashes or end up covered in welts."

Eirlys made a little grimace, accompanied by a soft *eew* and Penny laughed.

"No, it wouldn't look good on us."

"Wouldn't look good on them, either," muttered Eirlys.

"She also used to mix up love potions, as I recall," said Mrs. Lloyd. "You know the sort of thing. Two drops of this, a bit of chopped-up that, shake well, slip into his drink, and he's guaranteed to fall in love with you."

Penny and Eirlys laughed.

Mrs. Lloyd hesitated for a moment and then joined in. "Well, she always was a little bit away with the fairies. Some folks thought she was as daft as brush. Daft Dilys some folk used to call her." Mrs. Lloyd hesitated for a moment. "Me, I always thought there was something rather sly and secretive about her."

"I'm surprised I haven't heard about this Dilys or even run into her," said Penny as Eirlys applied a top coat to Mrs. Lloyd's nails. "Where does she live?"

"Do you know, I'm not really sure," said Mrs. Lloyd. "But she's quite likely staying with her brother. He used to be one of the gardeners up at Ty Brith Hall back when it was a going concern. Emyr's mother used to say what he didn't know about gardening wasn't worth knowing. And then when he got sick last spring, Alzheimer's maybe, or something like that, Rhys Gruff-ydd let him stay on in his little cottage up there, even though he couldn't work anymore."

Mrs. Lloyd took a sip of the tea Penny had asked Rhian to bring her.

"As for running into her, if Dilys doesn't want you to see her, you won't. She keeps to the back ways and stays well out of sight. She was always like that, as I recall. Creeping about in the woods and sometimes by moonlight, too."

Mrs. Lloyd looked at her watch.

"Anyway, if you're all that interested in these two, why don't you have a word with your Gwennie? She worked up at the Hall practically her whole life and her mother before her. She'll know as much about that pair as anyone would."

Thirteen

A few minutes later, her manicure finished, Mrs. Lloyd prepared to leave. "I wasn't sure if I should mention this or not, Penny, as I'm sure it's a bit of a sore spot with you, but I noticed the new nail bar and tanning salon has opened. I do hope it won't impact your business too much, really I do."

She smiled at Penny. "I hope you know you'll always have my support. I won't be setting foot in that place. I hear some of those nail bars run by foreigners don't clean their tools very well and you can pick up all kinds of nasty infections."

She gave a little shudder. "No, don't bother. I'll see myself out. I know the way."

Penny and Eirlys exchanged glances and Eirlys nodded.

"I'll be sure to sterilize them properly, Penny. I always do."

She gathered up the tools, set them on a tray and then, using a disinfectant cloth, she wiped down her work surface and laid a clean white towel over it.

"You know, Penny, what Mrs. Lloyd just said got me thinking. If you weren't a nice person and you wanted to hurt your rival's business, you could—"

Penny held up a hand to stop her. "Eirlys, I'm surprised at you, to even think such a thing." *I'm surprised at myself, too, then, thought Penny. For thinking the same thing.*

"But, Eirlys, that gives me an idea. Let's check the schedule, and if you haven't got another customer booked just now, I'd like you to do something for me."

Twenty minutes later, Eirlys pushed open the door to the Handz and Tanz salon.

Unlike the Llanelen Spa, which was decorated in calm, soothing pastels, giving it a sophisticated air of clean tranquility, Handz and Tanz was a riot of hot neon pinks and lime greens that glowed garishly bright under fluorescent lighting. Loud rock music played in the reception area, where an unsmiling Asian receptionist looked up as Eirlys entered.

"I'd like to book a manicure, please," Eirlys said, raising her voice to be heard over the music.

"When you like to come in?" the receptionist asked.

"How about tomorrow?"

"What time?"

"Two o'clock."

Eirlys looked around the salon while the receptionist made a show of thumbing through an appointment book with very few entries in it. Two young Asian girls dressed in bright pink smocks smiled shyly at her.

"What your name?"

"Eirlys."

"How you spell?"

As Eirlys spelled her name, the receptionist printed it slowly in her appointment book. She then handed Eirlys a card with the date and time written on it.

"You want tanning?" the receptionist asked. "We have opening special."

"No, no thanks. No tanning."

"You want pedicure? Opening special."

As Eirlys was about to reply, raised voices coming from a back room caught their attention. All eyes turned toward the door as a woman, swiping at her eyes with her hand, emerged and, without looking at them, pushed her way out the front door. A small Asian man glared at the women in the pink smocks and then said something to them in a language Eirlys did not understand. They lowered their eyes immediately, and with one last hard stare he disappeared into the back room. No one spoke in the brief embarrassed silence he left in his wake, and then Eirlys asked the receptionist, "Could I have a price list, please?"

The woman handed her a photocopied list of services. After thanking her, Eirlys added, "I was wondering, I hope you don't mind me asking, but are you Chinese?"

The receptionist shook her head but didn't look up. "Vietnamese."

The two young women in the pink smocks nodded and smiled and began talking excitedly to each other.

"Well?" said Penny when Eirlys returned.

"I don't think we have to worry too much about Handz and

Tanz, Penny," said Eirlys, handing her the price list. "They don't charge as much as we do, but there were no customers and the atmosphere is terrible." She described the argument between the man and woman and then added, "I think anyone who would go there would not be someone who would come to us, so I don't think we'll lose any of our customers to them." And then: "In fact, now that I think about it, I don't know who they're in business to serve. Older women like Mrs. Lloyd wouldn't dream of going there, and everyone my age likes coming to us."

"They may cater to women who like artificial nails and tanning, so you might be right about them not appealing to our clients," said Penny. "But tell me about the crying woman. What did she look like?"

She listened and then nodded. "That must have been Mai, the woman who came here that day to tell us the nail bar was opening. I wonder who the man is, though. Gareth told me her husband is English." Eirlys shrugged.

"What should I do about the manicure I booked for tomorrow?"

"Cancel it. We're not giving them any of our money, and if you want a manicure, I'll give you one after work tonight." She picked up the ends of Eirlys's fingers and looked at her nails. "Yes, you could do with one.

"Right. Now, can you take over from Rhian while she goes to lunch? I need a word with Gwennie."

"Oh, her." Gwennie bent over and tossed a few more towels into the washing machine in the laundry area on the ground floor behind the kitchen. "I haven't heard that name in a long time. Dilys Hughes. She must be in her seventies now. Daft as a brush, folk used to say about her. All that nonsense with her twigs and berries."

She set the controls on the machine and straightened up as the wash cycle began.

"If you're ill, see a doctor, is what I say. That's what they're for and they know a sight more than she does. That's what they go to school for. And for a long time, too."

She reached into the dryer, pulled out an armful of towels and set them on her wooden folding table.

"Why are you asking about her?"

"Because Mrs. Lloyd told me this morning she's returned to the area. Apparently she's been gone for years. Says she thinks Dilys is living in a tied cottage up at Ty Brith Hall with her brother."

Gwennie rested her small hands on the soft pile of white towels.

"So she's back, is she? Well, that is interesting."

"Why is it interesting, Gwennie?"

"Well, her brother, Pawl, who was the head gardener at Ty Brith for years, he was courting that woman Juliette Sanderson, who turned up dead in the ductwork of our Spa. And Dilys disappeared or left the area about the same time as Juliette went missing. I hadn't thought about that for years. It was hearing her name again that reminded me of that connection, I guess."

"Gwennie, tell me. Exactly where is this cottage? I want to talk to them."

"You can try, I suppose, Miss Penny, but you might not get much sense out of either of them."

71

"Well, look, can you draw me a little map of where I would find their cottage? Ty Brith is a big place."

"Go on the bus, will you?"

"Yes, I'll have to. Victoria's not here to come with me and she's the one who drives."

"Right, well, you want to get off at the stop after the one at the bottom of the road that leads up to the Hall. If you give me a piece of paper, I'll draw a map of how to get to the cottages the back way through the woods so you won't be seen from the house."

Penny dashed into the photocopier room next door and returned with a piece of paper from the recycling bin. "Here, use the back of that," she said, handing Gwennie the piece of paper and pulling a pen out of her pocket.

Gwennie started to sketch the route Penny should take, and then paused.

"I was meaning to speak to you, Miss Penny, about the laundry facilities. I don't like the clothes dryer. I was wondering if we could have a drying rack installed. These are nice towels we've got and they'll last longer if they're air-dried. And when spring comes, we really should hang them up outside. They might be a little crispier, but it'll be better for them in the long run. And the clients will love the way they smell."

"Yes, Gwennie, that's a great idea. Of course we can. And we'll save on the electricity costs, too."

At the end of the day, Penny double-checked to see that the alarm was armed, then locked the Spa door behind her, stepping out into the cold, clear evening. She had left Eirlys in charge for the next morning so she could go to Ty Brith Hall in search of

Dilys Hughes and her brother, Pawl. She wished Victoria were here to come with her. So much had happened that she would have loved to discuss with her friend. But Victoria had e-mailed to say she'd be home next week, and Penny couldn't wait to see her.

Fourteen

Llanelen changes instantly from town to country. There is no gradual transition from urban architecture to rural landscape. There's one last stone house and, beside it, rolling farmland, where horses and sheep spend their days grazing in peaceful coexistence. The landscape surrounding the town is steeped in the natural beauty of the British countryside—woodlands, deciduous forests, narrow winding roads edged with grey stone fences that hem in lush green pastures and meadows, hedgerows that shelter small birds and animals, and everywhere, an abundance of plants, shrubs, and trees. To the casual observer, that's all they are—plants, shrubs, and trees. But to Dilys Hughes, they were an endless, always open pharmacy of herbs and botanicals. The cure for everything that ailed man or beast—baldness, insomnia, gout, acne, lameness, depression, unrequited love, aching muscles, and so much more—was right there for the picking, if only you knew where to look and what to choose. And Dilys did. She spent her days foraging along the roadsides and across the fields with the handwoven basket she'd used for decades over her arm, cutting leaves of sorrel here and digging up dandelion roots a little farther on.

She dressed the same in all weathers: a long, black waterproof coat over a tattered green cardigan and, beneath that, layers of grey nondescript clothing. Her hands were always gloved, covered in the soil that gave life to the leaves she loved. The soles of her old boots, tied on with broken laces, were caked with sheep dung, mud, and dried bits of grass and dead leaves.

No one knew where she had been or what she'd been doing for all the years she'd been gone from Llanelen. One day she was gone, and decades later she was back. It was as simple as that

She'd promised their mother a long time ago that if anything should happen to her brother, she'd take care of him. So when she'd sensed that something was not right with him, burdened with painful memories and now well into her seventies, she had come home.

The next morning, clutching Gwennie's map, Penny stepped off the bus at the stop Gwennie recommended and walked a few feet along the side of the road, looking for the path indicated on the map that would lead to the Ty Brith cottages where the Hughes brother and sister lived. The cottages, Gwennie had told her, were located behind a small wooded area, adjacent to the now unused stable block.

A light wind ruffled her hair as she walked steadily along the path, which rose at a slight incline. The ground, littered with last year's frost-crisped leaves, was firm beneath her feet. Patches of snow lay beneath the trees where the sun, too feeble as yet, had not been able to reach them. But the silent, brown winter landscape was beginning to soak up the light, and in open sunny spots a scattering of snowdrops displayed their milky-white, bell-shaped flowers. Penny paused for a moment to admire them and then pushed on. A few minutes later the woodland gave way to a small clearing. Ahead of her was the wooded area that separated the grey stone buildings of the stables and outbuildings from the three terraced cottages built in the same grey stone. Beyond the little woodland, the peaked outline of the roof of the main house, Ty Brith Hall, was silhouetted against a bright blue sky. Smoke curled out of the four chimneys and then, caught by the breeze, drifted over the valley until it disappeared.

Penny walked behind the cottages until she reached the one on the end closest to the path that led to the Hall. She thought she heard voices coming from inside, so she made her way along the side of the house, and with a quick glance in the direction of Ty Brith Hall, she knocked on the front door. The voices inside fell silent.

While she waited, she studied the small sign mounted on the wall of the cottage beside the door frame. Etched in slate were the words Y BWTHYN BACH. The Little Cottage.

She knocked again and heard low, urgent voices. A moment later the door scraped open a few inches.

"Yes? What do you want?"

"Are you Dilys Hughes?"

"What if I am?"

"My name is Penny Brannigan and I'd like to talk to you."

"What about?"

"About someone who worked at Ty Brith Hall a long time ago."

The door opened a little wider, revealing a woman with dark, pinched eyes, thin lips, long grey hair, and a shapeless brown felt hat pulled low over her ears. She wore an outdoor coat and fingerless gloves.

"I know you," she said. "I've seen you around and about. You do that thing with pencils." She moved her hand back and forth in rapid strokes.

"That's right," said Penny. "Sketching. Yes, I do." The woman leaned closer, giving off a surprisingly pleasant odor that seem to combine the old-fashioned scents of lavender and violets with clothes that had recently been mothballed. The woman peered into Penny's face.

"You're not sleeping," she said. "I'll give you something."

Penny started to protest, but Dilys repeated, "I'll give you something. You'd better come in. Mind your head."

She pushed the door open, stepped back and waited. "I've just come in from one of my rambles. Give me a minute to take my coat off and wash my hands and I'll be right with you."

It took a moment for Penny's eyes to adjust to the gloom, but when they did, she saw that the front door opened onto a small hallway with a kitchen on the right and a room that served as sitting room on the left. Every inch of wall and surface was covered with something either decorative or useful. Old books and coloured bottles jostled for space on shelves and tables. Plants hung upside down from the low, blackened ceiling beams to dry. The room smelled of the passing of time. The dust on the deep-set windowsills mixed with the papery aroma of faded photographs, candle wax, and old wood.

In the dim light, she noticed an elderly man sitting in an armchair in the corner at the back of the room. His legs were covered with a tattered burgundy plaid blanket, its hem resting on a scuffed pair of brown carpet slippers. Patches of pink scalp, dotted with large brown spots, peeked through thin wisps of white hair. He regarded Penny with a mix of curiosity and childlike trust. He gave her a toothless smile and nodded. "Growing the herb," he said and tapped his nose.

"Oh, right," said Penny. "You must be Pawl. You used to be the gardener here, didn't you?"

He nodded and held up a bony hand. "Gardener. There's another one now. Not right." His head wagged from side to side.

"Take no notice of him," said Dilys as she returned to the room and began weighing out dried leaves. "So tell me. What brings you here?"

Penny reached into her pocket and pulled out a copy of a black-and-white photograph that Detective Sergeant Bethan Morgan had given her a few months earlier of the woman whose body had been found in the ductwork of the Llanelen Spa during the renovation. The photo had been found among the effects of an American man who had died at Conwy Castle just before Christmas.

It showed a young woman holding the hand of a small boy dressed in shorts and a Fair Isle vest and wearing sturdy boots. He smiled awkwardly at the camera, as if the photographer had told him to. The woman gazed down benignly at the boy, her face lit up from within as if by love.

Behind them was a closed wooden door, set into a sturdy

stone frame with rosebushes growing up each side. On the door was a knocker in the shape of a dolphin. It was without question the back door of Ty Brith Hall.

Penny hesitated for a moment and then handed the photo to Dilys Hughes. "Do you recognize that woman? She used to work here. Can you tell me anything about her?"

Dilys set a small packet down on her worktable and turned to Penny. She took the photo and glanced at it. Her eyes slid over to her brother, who was gazing out the high-set window over the fields, seemingly lost in his own world. He raised a cup of tea to his lips and took a loud slurp.

"We knew her," Dilys said in a low voice. "She worked in the kennels here. Looked after the dogs. Pawl wanted to marry her. Her name was Juliette Sanderson." Pawl Hughes let out a sudden, loud cry that startled both women. Dilys dropped the photograph, which fluttered to the floor. As she bent over to pick it up, her brother caught sight of it and tensed. In an instant he was transformed from a mild, friendly man into one filled with rage. As a great fury welled up within him, he threw his half-empty cup at his sister. His hands were clenched in fists of rage as he tried to strike out at her. "You, you, you," he bellowed, as a trail of spittle dripped from one corner of his mouth.

"You'd better go now." Dilys glanced at her brother and then picked up the small packet wrapped in brown paper and tied with purple string she had set down on her worktable a few moments earlier. "It's just enough for a few nights," she said, handing it to Penny. "If you want more, and I expect you will, you can come back. I'll be ready for you." As she accepted the packet, Penny was startled by the appearance of Dilys's hand.

The skin was taut and smooth. There were no liver spots or

any other signs of aging. It looked like the hand of a much younger woman, younger by decades.

She touched Penny's arm and gave her a firm push toward the door. "My photo," said Penny.

Dilys reached over, picked it up off the floor, and gave it to Penny. "Here, take it."

"Your hands. Can I ask you what you use . . ."

But with a gentle pressure Penny found herself outside and the door closed firmly behind her.

Fifteen

She arrived at the Spa to be greeted by a smiling Rhian. "I've just been copied on an e-mail Victoria sent you," she said. "Change of plan. She's coming home early. She's due to arrive at Manchester tomorrow and should be here by teatime." She grinned at Penny. "I expect you'll be glad to see her."

"Oh, won't we all. Things can get back to what passes for normal around here." Penny paused. "Have you got the key to her flat? We should get in a few basics for her—milk and a packet of biscuits—so she can at least have a nice cup of tea when she arrives home."

"I'll sort that out on my lunch hour tomorrow," said Rhian. "And some fresh bread and cheese and thin-sliced ham. And tomatoes. And yogurt, too. That Greek kind she likes."

"Good idea," said Penny. "I'll leave you to take care of all that, then. I think I'll just see how everyone else is getting on, and then I'll be in my office if you need me. I've got some spreadsheets that need updating and they take ages to do. You know what Victoria's like. She'll want to see them first thing."

She glanced in the manicure room, where Eirlys was busy with a customer. The doors to the treatment rooms were closed, indicating the masseur and beautician were with clients, so she didn't disturb them. She peered in the hair salon, where Alberto, their recently hired hairdresser, was trimming a woman's hair. Penny watched as he held the hair between two fingers and, using his fingers as a guide, carefully snipped the ends. Their eyes met in the mirror above the customer's head and they exchanged smiles.

"All right?" Penny asked.

Alberto nodded.

Penny then locked eyes in the mirror with the dark brown ones of Alberto's client.

"Hello, Mai," she said, entering the room and placing a hand on the woman's shoulder. "I'm so terribly sorry about your daughter."

"Thank you. You must think this very strange, me being here, but I needed a trim and just didn't have the energy or imagination to go anywhere else. I hope you don't mind."

"No, of course not. Not at all." *Your money is as good as the next person's,* thought Penny.

"I've been wanting to speak with you. To ask you some questions. Not about business. When we finish here, would it be all right if I spoke to you? In private, if you don't mind?"

"Yes, of course. Just let Rhian, our receptionist, know when you're ready. I'll be in my office and she'll show you in. I'll see you there." She raised an inquisitive eyebrow at Alberto. "About twenty minutes," he said as he ran his fingers through his client's hair to get a sense of whether the ends were equal.

"That's good enough," Mai told him. "I don't want it any shorter."

Alberto reached for his blow-dryer.

Penny looked up to see Mai standing in the doorway of her office. "We have a quiet room down the hall," said Penny. "Let's go there." They slipped into the room and sat down in the chocolate-brown chairs, facing each other. Penny leaned forward, clasping her hands between her knees, and waited.

"Well, first, I need a bit of practical help," Mai began. "I need domestic help up at the Hall. I can't manage that great big place on my own. Do you know anyone who could do a bit of cleaning and that sort of thing? The woman who used to be there decided not to stay on."

That would be Gwennie, who now works for me, thought Penny, and no, she won't be going to work for you.

"No, I'm sorry, but I don't know anyone. Have you tried advertising locally? Or even in *The Lady*? That's the place to get domestic help, I believe."

Mai shook her head. "I thought you might know someone who could use a few hours' work for a good wage. With both my children gone, you'd think I'd have more time, but I can't seem to . . ."

Mai struggled to compose herself.

"I am not doing well," she said. "It's a terrible thing to lose a child. I had to identify the body. All the way there I kept hoping

85

it wouldn't be her. And then to finally see her, lying there. Seeing what I knew to be true but not wanting it to be true. Thinking this is my daughter, dead. But how can it be?"

She lifted her eyes to Penny and then looked away quickly.

"I can't sleep. I can't focus on my work. I don't care about the new shop. My son spends most of his time now in Birmingham, although he comes and goes. Sometimes he's here and sometime's he's not. I never know where he is or when he'll turn up. I've lost control of him. I'm very afraid of the crowd he's with in Birmingham, but I can't get through to him. My life is in ruins." Her eyes filled with tears. "You must think it very strange that I would come here and tell you all this, but as you see, I'm desperate."

"Did you want me to help find out who killed Ashlee?"

Mai looked surprised. "No, why would I want you to do that? The police will do that."

Penny raised her hands in a fluttering gesture. "Oh, I'm sorry, it's just that I've been involved in solving a murder before, so I thought when you said you were desperate that you . . ."

Shaking her head, Mai said, "No, sorry. I don't know anything about that. It's just that the police told me it was you who found the body. I thought it might help me if you would tell me how you came to find her." Her face looked thinner and older, as if crumpling from within. Her dark eyes seemed shot through with pain. "Tell me everything you saw. Everything."

Penny nodded and described, as simply and tactfully as she could, how she and Alwynne had been sketching and Trixxi had led her to the body. "I knew right away who it was, I'm afraid, or at least I had a very strong sense that it was Ashlee because of the snakeskin manicure."

"So it was the manicure?"

"Yes, you see her right hand was exposed and I could see the fingernails. It was the snakeskin manicure I'd done earlier that week. So I told the police I was pretty sure I knew who it was. And I'm very sorry that it did turn out to be your daughter."

"Do you have children?"

"No, I don't," said Penny, "so I can only imagine what you must be going through."

"Well, multiply that by a hundred. By a thousand." She ran her fingers softly down her newly styled hair. "She was pregnant, you know."

"No, I didn't know."

"I don't understand that, either. She didn't have a boyfriend." She bit her lower lip. "I'm only telling you that because I wondered if maybe when she came to you for the manicure she might have said something to you about a boyfriend. I know from my own experience that clients will sometimes confide the most personal and intimate things when they're getting their nails done."

Penny shook her head. "No, she didn't say anything to me about a boyfriend. In fact, I even mentioned boys to her— something along the lines that she might meet a nice lad here in Llanelen—and she said she wasn't interested in boys."

"Then I don't understand why someone would want to kill her. It's beyond me why someone would have it in for her. What could she possibly have done? She was only nineteen. I told the police this. She had no enemies. In fact, as far as I knew, she barely had any friends."

She must have had at least one, thought Penny. A gentleman friend.

Sixteen

Victoria had left detailed instructions on how to close up and cash out at the end of the day, and while she'd been away, Rhian had taken care of that. But because Rhian had left early to keep a dentist's appointment, Penny was left to total up the day's takings and cash out. Most of the transactions were either credit card or debit. Entering codes on the device that processed credit card and debit transactions, she printed out a list of all the entries for the day. Then she took all the money out of the cash drawer, carefully counted back in fifty pounds for the next day's float, and added up the rest of the cash. There were only a couple of hundred pounds because most customers paid by debit or credit card, although Mai, she noted, had paid cash. She put the money, along with a deposit slip, in a grey canvas bag, filed the receipts, and switching on the alarm near the entrance to Victoria's flat, she let herself out the side door.

Even though she wasn't carrying a lot of money, she still felt nervous and would be glad when she had dropped the bag safely into the bank's night deposit slot. As she crossed the cobblestone square to the bank, a small figure emerged from Handz and Tanz. It seemed that he, too, was on his to way to deposit the day's takings. He made his way across the square, a large grey canvas bag tucked under his arm. It was about four times the size of the one Penny was carrying. Perhaps they don't take cards, Penny thought, or business must be booming. But she knew it wasn't. Except for a few girls lined up at a bus stop sporting the distinctive orange glow of a fake tan, she didn't know anyone who was patronizing the new place. And hadn't Eirlys said the place was empty? She watched from the shadows as the figure unlocked the night deposit collection box at the side of the bank, dropped in his bundle, and disappeared into the night. A few moments later she did the same and then set off through the quiet streets for the short walk to her cottage.

As she turned down a side street, a couple taping something to a lamppost caught her eye, and after hesitating for a moment, she crossed the street to see what they were doing. The young woman had clearly been crying. She smoothed a piece of paper around the post and held it while her companion taped it in place.

"It's our dog," the woman explained. "She's gone missing. Have you seen her?"

Penny looked at the poster, which featured a photo of a small black-and-white dog. "Her name's Katniss and we're desperate to get her back." The woman pointed to the phone number at the bottom of the poster. "If you do see her, please ring us on that number."

"I hope you find her," Penny said, adding she would certainly be on the lookout for the dog.

Glad to be home, Penny took Trixxi for a short walk, fed her, and then rummaged around in her fridge to see what she could find for her own dinner. She hadn't paid much attention to food in the past and her fridge often bordered on empty. But at Victoria's suggestion she had started to buy her groceries online, and now that they were delivered right to her door, she had no excuse for a bare pantry or barren refrigerator. She pulled a cheese and tomato quiche out of the freezer, set the oven to preheat, and wandered into her sitting room. She checked the phone. No messages. She picked up her handbag to sort through the papers she'd brought home and discovered the small parcel that Dilys Hughes had given her that morning. As she unwrapped the paper, a light fragrance escaped. She pushed the edges of the paper back and found a small muslin bag tied with a red ribbon. A little tag hung off it. She turned it over and read, *Lavender and verbena. Place near pillow for restful sleep.* The words were written in an old-fashioned script. She held the little bag to her nose and gave it a tentative sniff. It seemed quite nice, really. The package also contained an envelope. Written on it, in the same cramped handwriting, were the words *Valerian. For sleep. Mix one teaspoon in glass of warm water and take at bedtime. Do not exceed dosage in one night.* She set the parcel down and went to see to her dinner.

At bedtime, she placed the fragrant little bag near her pillow. The scent was soothing, she had to admit, and while she thought the lavender and verbena harmless enough, she decided not to

91

take the valerian. However, as the sleepless minutes ticked away into a frustrated hour, and then the beginning of another one, she got up and put the kettle on. I'll try just half a teaspoon with a cup of tea, she thought.

Seventeen

Stronger and a little earlier now, the morning light crept under the window blind, casting a steady beam of brightness across Penny's bed. She stirred and stretched, then looked at her bedside clock. Eight o'clock! She remembered taking a drink of the valerian brew and nothing after that. She must have slept right through the night. Instantly awake, and going over in her mind the list of things she needed to do to get ready for Victoria's return, she realized she felt more energetic and refreshed than she had in days. Weeks even.

"You look amazing," Penny told Victoria when she arrived home that afternoon. "Italy must have really agreed with you. Had a good time, then?"

"It was brilliant. I wasn't really ready to come back, but you have to go home sometime." Penny nodded. Victoria pushed a smart paper shopping bag across her desk. "Here, I brought you something back from Florence. I hope you like it."

"Oh, thank you!" Penny peeked into the bag, and pushing the white tissue paper aside, she pulled out a sleek black leather handbag. "It's beautiful," she said. "I love it."

"With your lifestyle, I'm not quite sure where you would wear it—it's not something you'd take sketching with you, but you might find a time and place for it," said Victoria. "Perhaps Gareth will take you to a dress-up kind of do where it would be appropriate."

"It's always good to have nice things," said Penny. "Our lives are so casual and underdressed now, but I'm sure I'll get good use of it." She smiled at her friend. "Thank you for thinking of me."

Victoria bobbed her head in acknowledgment as her eyes tightened and a bleak look flashed across her face.

"What's the matter, Victoria? You don't seem very pleased to be back. Did something happen out there? Eirlys thought you might have met someone."

"I did, actually," said Victoria. "He plays the cello."

She poured herself another cup of tea and then held up the teapot to Penny, who shook her head. "I love the cello. So mellow and mournful, all at the same time."

"But it was just a holiday romance, wasn't it?" asked Penny. "You're not thinking of packing it in here and moving out there to be with him, are you?"

Victoria set the teapot down.

"No, I'm not. I might have, possibly, had things been different, but . . ." She shook her head.

"What is it?" asked Penny. "What's the matter?"

"He's married."

"Ah."

"At first everything was wonderful and I was dying to tell you all about him, but then things just didn't seem right, so I confronted him with it. And then he admitted he's married and still living with his wife. He didn't think it was a big deal, but I sure did. How could I have been so naïve and stupid? As soon as I heard that, I finished with him and came home."

"And quite right, too. That kind of relationship is so dead end. Some women waste years on them. And he always treats the wife better. Makes you wonder."

Victoria shrugged. "I probably wasn't the first. Well, at our age most of the best ones are married, aren't they?" She added as an afterthought, "Or widowed. Like Gareth. Well, whatever, we all come with a lot of baggage, I guess."

Victoria was divorced and had invested her settlement in the Llanelen Spa.

"Well, enough about that. I don't want to waste one more minute of my life on him. Tell me the latest on what's been happening here. All the details. Don't leave anything out. Your e-mails were a little sketchy. I want to know how that new nail place is affecting our business."

So Penny began telling her what she knew of the new nail bar and tanning place.

"And when Eirlys dropped in, there were no customers. But I've seen a few young women, you know, in their early twenties, around town with that awful orange fake tan look. Honestly, do they think it makes them attractive? But anyway, here's the really weird thing. Last night, when I was making our cash deposit at the bank, I noticed someone coming out of the nail bar, and he had a cash deposit bag, too. It was at least three times the size of ours. How can that be, I asked myself. If the place was practically empty when Eirlys was there, what's the deal with all the cash? Where's it coming from?"

"Yes, I see what you mean." Victoria rubbed her chin. "Wait a minute. Have you seen a lot of men going in there? Maybe they're offering other services besides just the nails and tanning."

"You mean . . . ?" She thought for a moment. "Well, it's possible, I suppose, but no, I haven't seen a lot of men going in there. Haven't seen any, come to think of it, but there might be another door round the back, I suppose." She stood up. "I've had an idea and you might not like it. At least not at first."

"All right, let's hear it," said Victoria, as she took a sip of tea. "What?"

"Well, Mai, you know, the woman who owns the nail bar, was saying that she needed someone to come in and do a little light cleaning, and I thought that since she doesn't know about you and hasn't met you, that you could—"

"Oh, no," Victoria interrupted. "No, a thousand times, no. Never. It's not going to happen. No."

"Well, hear me out," said Penny. "I thought you could go up to the Hall for just an afternoon or two, and while you're doing the dusting, you could hear what they have to say and get a sense of what they're doing with their business. Where they're going with it. Who their customers are. Because there's something not quite right there and it could affect us. By us, I mean our business."

"So, you're suggesting a little industrial espionage."

"Well, if you want to call it that. Just until we get a better sense of what she's up to."

"I'll think about it. But I'm not sure I see the point. The people who live there aren't even likely to be at home in the afternoon, are they?"

Penny didn't answer. Instead, she scrabbled about in her bag. "I was in Llandudno the other day and you know that bargain shop at the end of Mostyn Street? I bought this for you." She handed over an old-fashioned pinafore that British char ladies had worn for decades. In a blue and white check pattern, it slipped on over the wearer's clothes, buttoned up the front and featured two large pockets.

Victoria eyed it with distaste.

"Do I have to?"

"Yes, you have to look the part, and we'll have to do something about your hair. You look much too good." Penny rubbed her hands together. "I know. We'll tie a kerchief around it."

"A kerchief! No one's worn a kerchief since the Second World War. I'll look like a land girl or like some woman you see in those old black-and-white documentaries working in a bomb factory."

Penny laughed.

"And what if she asks for references?" Victoria asked.

"She won't," said Penny, "because she's too desperate."

"Well, thanks very much for that."

"And anyway, I'll be recommending you, so that's a reference right there. So I'll ring her and let her know I've just thought of someone who might be able to do a little light cleaning. Oh, and why don't I say you're really good at cooking, too?"

Victoria groaned.

"Yes, she could start Monday morning," Penny said on the telephone a few minutes later. "Yes, she knows the way. Right, I'll tell her. Be there at nine." She pressed the button to end the phone call.

"You don't waste much time, do you?" said Victoria.

"Try the pinafore on," said Penny. "Go on, I want to see how you look in it. After all, it cost me five pounds, although I suppose that technically I could claim it as a business expense."

On Monday morning Victoria lifted the silver dolphin on the back door of Ty Brith Hall and gave two firm taps. A few moments later a small Asian woman opened the door and gestured Victoria inside. "Come in. The kitchen's this way."

Victoria, who had been to the house before and knew exactly where the kitchen was, said nothing and followed. "You can start by cleaning up the kitchen," Mai said, "and then dust and tidy up the downstairs rooms." Victoria looked around. The last time she had been in this room, back when Gwennie had worked at the Hall, the large, beautiful, country house kitchen had been immaculate. Trixxi's bed had been beside the Aga, a trug filled with freshly picked vegetables from the kitchen garden had been set down just over there, and the whole room had been filled with the delicious aroma of warm ginger biscuits.

Today, the room smelled of stale cigarette smoke. On the table, crushed cigarette ends spilled from an overflowing ashtray, and beside it was a tattered newspaper with a piece torn out of it. The rubbish hadn't been emptied for days, and the counter was littered with dirty dishes.

I don't need this, thought Victoria. This is disgusting. I don't have to be here and I don't have to do this.

She was about to tell Mai that she had changed her mind and would not be staying when a small, wiry Asian man entered the kitchen, followed by a tall, man with handsome, delicate features. His blond hair was combed back from his forehead and was all the same length, just scraping his collar. He sat at the table and gave Victoria a beaming smile, displaying unusually good teeth.

"Any chance of a cup of coffee, love?"

Before she could reply, Mai answered. "She's not here to make coffee for the likes of you, Bruno. She's here to tidy up. So leave her alone. She needs to get on with things."

"Well, you could help her out, then, by telling Derek not to smoke in the house. Where is he, by the way? Haven't seen him around lately. Not been up to anything he shouldn't, I hope."

The Asian man said a few words to Mai in a foreign language. She seemed to ignore him, replying to the blond man. "Where do you think he is? You're his best mate, Bruno, you should know. He's where he always is. Bloody great useless prat. Either in bed, down the pub, or at the bookies." The Asian man said something else that seemed to get Mai's attention. She turned to him, gestured at the blond man, and replied in what sounded like the same language.

Bruno smiled at Mai, shrugged, and then inclined his head in the direction of the Asian man. "He's your brother, love, and he runs the show. I just work for him."

As the two men prepared to leave, Mai turned her attention

to Victoria. "I've left your money in an envelope on the counter. When you've finished tidying up in here, please see to the front hall and the back corridor. They'll need mopping and the sitting room needs dusting. Do not go upstairs. Do not go into any of the outbuildings. There's nothing there that need concern you. Do you understand?"

Victoria nodded. "Good, well, you should be finished here by noon. You can let yourself out. Can you come back tomorrow? For the same number of hours? There are so many rooms here, it's impossible for me to look after them all, what with, well, everything. The dining room needs dusting and the main reception room at the front of the house. Could you do those tomorrow?"

To her surprise, Victoria heard herself agreeing to come back. She collected a few dirty dishes from the table, rinsed them, and squeezed them into the dishwasher. The ones on the counter would have to wait until the next load. She found some dishwasher powder under the sink and filled the little plastic compartment. She closed the door of the machine, locked it, and was just setting the dial when she heard voices in the downstairs corridor leading to the back door.

"The new gardener will be arriving tonight. Make sure you're here to let him in, and for God's sake, keep Derek well out of the way. Mai's asked me to go to Birmingham to check up on Tyler, so I'm not sure when I'll be back. I don't even know if I'll be able to find him. Keep an eye on Mai. Make sure she deposits the money. In fact, meet her at closing time and walk her to the bank. We wouldn't want anything to happen to it." That's the Vietnamese man, thought Victoria, Mai's brother. The accent was the same as Mai's but thicker, as if he hadn't tried as hard to learn English. Or maybe he hadn't been in the country as long. By now they were too far away for her to hear clearly what was being said, and then there was the faint sound of laughter just before the back door closed.

As the almost empty house settled into an uneasy silence, she glanced out the kitchen window that overlooked the car park and gardens and then carried on with her work.

Eighteen

I think you're right. There may be something going on up there," Victoria said to Penny over a late lunch of supermarket sandwiches in Penny's office. "He said something about a gardener arriving tonight, and making sure Mai deposits the money. From the nail bar, I guess."

Penny wiped her hands on a paper napkin and reached for her glass of water. "That's interesting about the gardener. Earlier this week I went to see the former head gardener at the Hall. He mentioned the word 'gardener,' too, and then got quite agitated when his sister started telling me about Juliette Sanderson." Penny described the visit to Dilys Hughes and her brother.

"Still, I'm not sure we really learned anything or if there was any point to your actually going up to the Hall today. What did Mai say, by the way, when you told her you wouldn't be coming back tomorrow?"

"Ah, well, that's the thing." Victoria grinned a little sheepishly.

"I told her I would be back tomorrow. She told me not to go into certain areas of the house and grounds, but I thought maybe if I go back I might be able to build a bit of trust and see what's happening."

"You do surprise me," said Penny. "I never would have expected you'd want to go back."

"Just curious, that's all." She started gathering up the wrappers from the sandwiches. "I'll put the kettle on, shall I, and then I've got a ton of e-mails to answer. Have you spoken to Gareth? I wondered what's the latest on Ashlee."

"I don't think that investigation's going very well. He's been looking into the family's affairs in Birmingham. He's coming back tonight, so maybe he'll have some news."

She thought for a moment.

"You know, the first day that Mai came here Mrs. Lloyd said something interesting. She couldn't understand why a family like that would buy Ty Brith Hall. They're not farmers, so it can't be the land they were after. I don't know if Mai has lady-of-the-manor pretensions, but she seems too busy running the nail bar and tanning place to be worrying about all that."

"Oh, you mean like in Victorian times when the lady would go visiting the poor with a basket over her arm, doling out jars of calf's foot jelly and meaty broth?" Victoria laughed.

"Yes," said Penny. "And opening the summer fete in a big flowery hat. But I haven't heard that they're active in the church or any other aspect of the community. Mrs. Lloyd says people really haven't taken to them at all. It's not that anyone's been rude or racist, but just not invited them anywhere or asked them to join anything."

"Well, why should people take to them? They live up there,

pretty much on their own, with a son who's run off back to Birmingham and a murdered daughter whose killer hasn't been found." Victoria summed it up.

"And really, it's none of our business what they get up to, is it?" asked Penny.

"No, I suppose it isn't."

"So we should probably just leave them alone."

"Yes, I expect we should. We've got a business to run. We've got better things to do."

A little silence fell over them as they mulled this over.

"Well, I'm still going back tomorrow," said Victoria. "In a funny kind of way I found it really interesting being there, listening to them talking amongst themselves. They took no notice of me. I'll see if there's anything to find out, and then I'll pack it in."

"Well, if you like it so much, why don't you leave it open, then?" suggested Penny. "In case you want to go back there later. Just tell her you can't come in for a bit, but don't actually quit."

Nineteen

"Now then, Eirlys, you're looking a little down today. Not your usual cheerful self. Everything all right?"

Eirlys shook her head and went on placing a few new bottles of nail polish on the shelves. She moved the bottles around, lining them up just so, paying attention to the order of the colours. She liked to group like with like, so all the corals were in one spot, the pinks in another, the novelty colours together, and so on.

Penny stayed where she was and gave Eirlys a few moments to get herself together.

Finally, she turned around and sighed.

"I don't know what to do, Penny. I can't tell my parents, but I think my brother is stealing. He's suddenly got new electronics and video games that he couldn't possibly afford. My parents haven't really noticed because they're so busy, but I'm very worried about him." Her eyebrows knit together. "I know you're friends with that policeman, so please don't tell him. I wouldn't want to get Trefor in trouble."

"No, of course you wouldn't. But you know for sure that he's stealing?" asked Penny.

Eirlys shook her head. "No, but I can't think of any other way he could be getting those things. He's got a brand-new smartphone. Where would he get the money for something like that? And how can he afford the monthly payments? I know my parents aren't paying for his phone plan."

"Has he picked up a part-time job after school?"

"Not that I know of. He hasn't said."

"Well, there's probably a simple explanation. We just don't know what it is yet." She smiled at her young assistant. "I hope he knows how lucky he is to have a big sister like you who cares so much about him."

Eirlys turned away and adjusted a few bottles of nail polish that were just fine where they were.

With Gareth due back from Birmingham that night, Penny decided to call in at the off-licence on her way home to pick up some beer and wine. As she rounded the corner into the cobblestone square, she noticed a small white dog tied up outside the supermarket, sitting on the pavement waiting for his owner. As she came a few steps closer, a hooded figure emerged from the street on the right side of the square, looked quickly around, then untied the dog and led him quickly away.

Thinking that something wasn't right, she hurried past the supermarket and looked down the street where the man had gone. She couldn't see him, so she continued on to the off-licence.

Twenty

DCI Gareth Davies took a long, appreciative drink of beer and then set the glass down. "I needed that." He smiled, taking Penny's hand. "How have you been? All right?"

"I haven't been sleeping very well," she said. "I start off all right, and then wake up in the middle of the night and can't get off again."

"Something bothering you?"

"Not really. Nothing more than usual." Penny shrugged. "You know how it is. Life. Usual stuff." She debated telling him about Dilys and then decided she would. "But I was given some valerian root and that seems to help."

"Valerian? Who gave you that?"

Penny told him how she'd been to talk to Dilys and her brother at Ty Brith Hall and how Dilys had given her an aromatic pillow and a small packet of dried herb with instructions on how to take it.

"Her brother used to be the head gardener at the Hall. He's got dementia now, Alzheimer's maybe, and she looks after him."

Davies closed his eyes and said nothing.

"How did you get on in Birmingham?" Penny asked. He opened his eyes and looked at her.

"We talked to the girl's friends and got nowhere. It's a very odd crime because we can't find a motive, but obviously someone must have had one."

"The baby's father?"

"We don't know who that was yet."

"Her mother told me she didn't have any boyfriends."

Davies raised an eyebrow.

"That's what I thought," said Penny. "There must have been someone in her life."

"We also looked into the mother's past. She was married before, to the children's father, a Vietnamese man from Lewisham, but it ended a few years ago and then she married the English fellow, Derek. He's known to the West Midlands police for minor things, and he does have a gambling problem."

"Mrs. Lloyd and I were wondering about the Hall. Why would people like that buy a big rural estate when they don't seem to have any interest in farming or running it? They don't seem suited to Ty Brith Hall, somehow. We had rather hoped that someone with a keen interest in organic gardening would take it on. It has so much potential."

Davies gave her a sharp look. "You might be on to something there." He shifted in his seat. "We'll be paying them another visit, anyway, so we'll try to take a look around."

He glanced at his watch. "What would you like to do about dinner?"

"Oh, I hadn't thought. I've got a few things in now that I'm better organized. How about some soup and a Welsh rarebit?"

"Sounds perfect. What can I do to help?"

"You could set the table. You know where the plates and cutlery are."

Settled at the dining room table, Gareth poured Penny a glass of wine. He had switched to water.

"One thing I did want to mention to you. We're seeing an increase in the number of reported dog thefts." Penny glanced over at Trixxi, asleep in front of the fire in the sitting room. "So don't leave her tied up outside a shop, even for a minute. 'I just popped in to get some milk,' the owner tells us, and when they come out, the dog's gone." He shook his head. "It's a terrible thing. They just can't believe their dog is gone." He took a sip of water. "And it's hell for the owner, wondering what might become of their pet." Penny put her spoon down and pushed her plate to one side.

"What are you saying, exactly?"

"Well, people wonder if their dog has been sold for medical research, for example." Sensing her distress, he did not elaborate on the far worse fates that befall some stolen pets. "But usually the dogs are just sold so someone can make a bit of fast money. They pretend they own the dog, say they can't look after it anymore, and sell it to an unsuspecting buyer. Mostly it's small dogs we've been hearing about. West Highland terriers, Maltese, that kind of dog.

"Still, we want to get the word out, so you should tell any of your clients who own dogs to be careful. We'll also be issuing a press release so the media can run the story."

111

He smiled at her. "It may be that the women with small dogs who come to your Spa carry them about in their handbags."

Penny made a little strangling noise, set down her fork, and looked at her hands.

"I've got an awful feeling I saw a dog being taken today. There was a small white dog, tied up outside the supermarket, and then a man came and led it away."

"Did you get a look at him? Can you describe him?"

Penny shook her head. "He was wearing a dark-coloured hoodie and moved fast, so I think he was young. If it was a he, of course."

Davies reached for his phone. "I'll call Bethan to see if it was reported. And we'll get the CCTV tapes."

A minute later he ended the call.

"A Maltese?"

"Could have been. Something like that. White and fluffy."

"We did have one reported missing today from outside the supermarket, I'm sorry to say."

"Something about it didn't seem right at the time, and I've just realized what it was. It wasn't so much that the man didn't come directly out of the shop to get the dog but came along the street. It was that the dog didn't wag his tail. Whenever I leave Trixxi for a few minutes, she wags her tail when she sees me."

Penny brushed her hair back from her forehead.

"Something at the time didn't feel right. I tried to follow him and looked down the street that leads off the square where they'd gone, but they'd disappeared." She gave him a defeated look. "I feel terrible."

"Never mind, love, you weren't to know. And you did try to follow them, even though you didn't know what was really going on. That's more than most folk would have done."

They finished their meal and settled in to watch a new game show. Penny liked to call out the answers, while Gareth made uncomplimentary remarks about the contestants' mental abilities. "That's the beauty of watching a game show on telly," he said. "It's always your turn and you are always so much smarter than the contestants. And there's never any pressure." But tonight their hearts just weren't in it, and a gloomy, tired pall hung over them as they sat close on the sofa, her head resting on his shoulder and his arm around her.

As a full moon rose over Llanelen, Pawl Hughes stirred in his sleep. In the close darkness, in the small room where he had slept every night of his adult life, he found familiarity and peace that comforted him after the confused turmoil of a day spent struggling to understand and remember. In his dreams he was once again young and fit, and as a spectator, he watched himself from afar doing the ordinary things he used to do. Oh, look, that's me planting out the beans in the kitchen garden, and there I am cutting the pale pink roses that Emyr's mother, the lady of the house, loves so much. He heard the faint sound of dogs barking, reminding him of the beautiful girl who worked in the kennels, looking after the black Labs that were born and bred on the estate. He heard her laughing, but as his eyes opened in the dove-grey light before dawn, he told himself it was a dream. Just a dream. He closed his eyes and sank back into oblivion, the dream already forgotten as moon-washed shadows crept over his bed, carrying him toward morning.

Twenty-one

*P*enny stirred and came awake. She didn't need to look at her bedside clock to know dawn was approaching. She lay back, knowing she'd get up in a few minutes because she would not be able to get back to sleep. She'd used up the sample of valerian Dilys Hughes had given her, and although lurking at the back of her mind was a fear that she might be becoming dependent on it, she wanted more. I'll go and see her first thing, she thought, as she threw back the covers and groped about on the floor with her feet, looking for her slippers.

In the sunny kitchen of the rectory Bronwyn Evans frowned at the screen on her laptop. The church bulletin for Sunday's service had to be done by noon on Friday, and while she normally managed to get most of it written on Thursday, she was determined that this week she'd have it all done, or most of it, anyway, early so she and Thomas could enjoy a day out with Robbie on Friday.

She glanced at the time in the corner of her computer screen. Just another half hour, three quarters at most, she thought, should do it. Her cairn terrier, Robbie, which she had found shivering and near death in the cemetery last year and then adopted, wagged his tail and went to the back door.

"Just a minute, Robbie, and then I'll take you out," Bronwyn said. He barked again and this time she understood the urgency.

"Oh, all right." She got up and opened the kitchen door. She'd let him out into the rectory garden on his own many times before, and he'd bark when he was ready to come back in.

She returned to her laptop and began work on the announcements for the week. Prayers for dear Mary Williams, who lived alone in her lovely old seventeenth-century cottage and who was feeling poorly but getting better; the mother's meeting is canceled; a reminder that gently used clothing and household goods were needed for the spring jumble sale. She called up the Internet to search for a photo that would suit the jumble sale item and spent a few minutes, longer than she meant to, on that task. The Internet is such a black hole, she thought. But since I'm here anyway, I might as well renew my library books and see if they've got in anything new I might like.

As her mind drifted away to what her husband, Thomas, might like for lunch, she reached out for a scrap of paper and wrote a short shopping list: carrots, balsamic vinegar, milk. There was something else, but she couldn't think what it was. She went to the refrigerator, opened the door, and surveyed the contents. Moving a few items around, she peered to the back. She opened a drawer and pulled out a few wilted leaves of lettuce. That's it. She returned to her desk and added lettuce to her shopping list, and after a moment's thought, she added tomatoes.

She glanced again at the clock on her computer screen. That's odd, she thought, Robbie should have been barking to be let in by now. Maybe he's got into something he shouldn't have in the cemetery.

She slipped on her coat and opened the door that led to the rectory garden. Situated alongside the River Conwy, the garden was open to all and people had to pass by it on their way to the church and cemetery.

Calling Robbie's name, Bronwyn walked down the path that led to the church. She checked behind the tombstones in the cemetery as an increasing sense of panic began to swell within her.

"Robbie!" she called. "Robbie, come!" She prayed that her fears were unfounded and in a moment he'd come bounding out from behind a weathered tombstone, tail wagging furiously, and run up to her and put his muddy paws on her leg.

But he didn't. After she'd retraced her steps all over the cemetery and garden, a dreadful twist of fear settled in her stomach.

She ran back to the rectory and, throwing open the door, called out, "Thomas, Thomas, it's our Robbie. I can't find him. I think he's gone."

Penny gulped in some cleansing breaths of cold air as she climbed the last stretch before entering the small clearing that backed onto the row of workmen's cottages at the far end of the Ty Brith estate. The sweet sound of birdsong filled the air.

The ground was beginning to thaw and felt slightly spongy under the soles of her hiking boots. Trixxi trotted beside her, occasionally wandering off to explore something that caught her attention and then returning to Penny's side. As she neared the cottage, she clipped the lead to Trixxi's collar, and a moment later she knocked on the door.

As before, Dilys opened it.

"I knew you'd be back," she said. "Folks get to like and depend on my medicinals. You'd better come in, then. The dog's all right."

Penny stepped in, keeping a tight hold on Trixxi's lead. As her eyes adjusted to the dimness, she saw Pawl sitting in his chair at the back of the overheated room. He leaned forward and then let out a loud, joyful cry. He gestured at Trixxi and called, "Nelly. Nelly." Dilys looked up from her workbench, where she had started weighing out dried leaves on a small kitchen scale. "Take no notice of him. He thinks your dog is another dog he used to know. They used to call all the pups in the same Ty Brith litters names that started with the same letter, so Nelly was from the *N* litter. What's your dog called?"

"Trixxi."

Dilys leaned over and looked at her. "Mind you, all black dogs look pretty much the same to me and I'm no judge of dog flesh, but by any chance is she a Ty Brith dog? Was she born and bred on the estate, do you know?"

"As a matter of fact, she was, so I guess she would have been from the *T* litter. She used to belong to Emyr Gruffyd himself. It's a long story how she came to be with me, but Emyr is away a lot just now and he couldn't have her with him." Penny leaned over and gave Trixxi a pat. "Your brother seems to like her. Would he like to pat her, do you think?"

"I expect he would." Penny led Trixxi over to Pawl and he reached out his arms to the dog as she approached. Trixxi wagged her tail, sniffed at his knee, then raised her dark brown eyes to Penny, seeking direction.

"Hello, Pawl," said Penny. "This is Trixxi. She was born here at Ty Brith." Pawl smiled at the dog. "Trixxi," he repeated. "Trixxi, hmm, born here." As Pawl began to stroke her shiny black fur, Trixxi turned back toward him and he ran his hands gently down the length of her. His large hands were lined with heavy blue veins and showed the final effects of long summers spent working outdoors. Trixxi seemed to be enjoying the attention as he continued patting her. "Water?" he asked. "Trixxi?"

"That's a good idea," Penny said. "I'm sure she'd love a drink."

"I'll get it," said Dilys. "Just let me finish up here." Trixxi yawned and sank slowly to the floor at Pawl's feet. Pawl picked up a watch from the table beside him and examined it. He turned it over and ran his fingers down the strap. He pinched his lips together and set the watch back down on the table. Penny was unsure if she should offer to help him put it on. Before she could do or say anything, Dilys came over to them, carrying a deeply crackled pudding basin which she set down on the floor near Trixxi. Trixxi got to her feet and began to drink. As she did, Pawl pointed at her. "Nelly," he said, with a hopeful smile. "No, that's not Nelly," Dilys told him. "That's Trixxi." She turned to Penny. "He thinks she's Nelly from long ago and who can blame him? They all look the same to me, those black Labs."

She walked over to her worktable under the window and picked up a small packet, which she held out to Penny.

"Here you go, then."

Penny took the packet from her. "I didn't really want to come here, you know," she said. "But I found the valerian really helped me sleep. I'm worried, though, that I might become dependent on it."

"It's all natural," said Dilys. "It won't hurt you."

Penny handed her a ten-pound note. "I hope you'll accept this," she said. "I hope that's enough. I wasn't sure how to handle the money aspect. If it costs more, please let me know."

Dilys took it and tucked it in her pocket. "Most welcome. We just have our small pensions."

"I was wondering about that," said Penny. "It's good that the new owners have let you stay on here. For a peppercorn rent, I hope."

"New owners? What new owners?"

"The people who bought the Hall from Emyr Gruffydd. They've let you stay on, have they?"

"Them?" She made a little moue of disgust. "They don't own the property. They rent it. Mr. Emyr himself came to tell us we'd be allowed to stay on. He told them that's the way it would be, and it's written into the rental agreement that Pawl and I can live here as long as we like."

She shifted uneasily and glanced toward the Hall. "In fact, I wouldn't be surprised if it was really Mr. Emyr's father, Mr. Rhys that would be, who decided we'd be allowed to live in the cottage for Pawl's lifetime. He was a wonderful man, he was. Very fair to the people who worked for him, and he valued their loyalty. He treated everyone well." She sighed. "People have no idea what it was like back then. We were one big happy family here at Ty Brith Hall. And so self-sufficient. Just about everything that needed doing we did for ourselves. We raised all our own animals, grew all our own fruits and vegetables, made all our own wine and beer. There was even a dairy where they turned milk and cream into beautiful cheeses."

"So what about the other cottages in the terrace?" asked Penny. "Does anyone still live in any of them? Do you have any neighbours, in case you need anything?"

Dilys shook her head. "No, we're all right as we are." She inclined her head in the direction of the main house. "They keep themselves to themselves and so do we, and that's the way we like it.

"Sometimes Pawl thinks he hears someone moving about next door, but he's just thinking about the old days. He can remember things from long ago but has no memory of the present. He won't even remember you were here."

"But all things considered you're managing all right, are you? Is there anything you need?"

"What's with all this social worker talk?" Dilys stiffened and Penny realized she'd asked too many questions.

"I'm so sorry. I didn't mean to pry. I just want to help, if I can."

"We don't need your help, thanks all the same." Dilys folded her arms to indicate that the conversation was over.

"Yes, well, I'm sorry. I'll just get Trixxi and we'll be on our way."

As Penny picked up her lead, Trixxi got to her feet and trotted over to the door. Dilys placed his old plaid blanket over Pawl's knees, told him she was going out for a bit and that he was to stay where he was and not get into any bother.

He smiled up at her and then picked up the watch. He turned it over in his hands as if he'd never seen it before.

"Juliette gave him that watch," Dilys said in a low voice. "He treasures it, but he can't remember why. I don't think he even knows what it is or what it's for, but he has a great attachment to it."

"That's interesting," said Penny. "He remembers that it's precious to him—that it has significance in his life—but he can't remember why."

"Exactly," said Dilys as she slung a leather carrier bag over her shoulder and pulled the door shut behind them.

"If you've got a moment," said Penny when they were outside, "I'd like to have a closer look at the cottages." She stepped back to take in the three houses, solidly built of grey stone, each one joined to its neighbour by the side walls. The houses seemed the same, except . . .

"The houses on each end are slightly bigger," Dilys said, interrupting Penny's thought. "Pawl was given an end one when he became head gardener and the one at the other end"—she gestured toward it—"that was where the cook and her husband lived. He was a carpenter. Did odd jobs about the place. The rest of the staff lived in the main house or above the stables. A few lived out."

Penny swept her eyes one last time across the cottages' façade, admiring their symmetry and strength. "I'd like to come back and paint the cottages," she said, adding, "Yours is the only one that has a window box."

"Yes," said Dilys. "Pawl used to be in charge of all the gardens on the estate. The rose garden, vegetables, orchard, cutting garden, everything. Mysterious, beautiful things happen in gar-

122

dens, he used to say. He saw every tomato as a miracle. Now"—she gestured at the wooden box filled with nothing but dirt on the ledge outside the sitting room window—"that's his garden."

She shrugged, then hoisted the strap of her leather carrier bag across the other shoulder so it crossed over her body.

"I wanted to ask you about your hands," Penny said. "I couldn't help but notice how youthful they look. I wondered what you've done to take care of them."

Dilys glanced down at her hands, now covered in gloves. "Well, first, I never let the sun on them. Even in summer I wear gloves. And then, of course, I've used my special hand cream for decades. I make it myself."

"I wonder if I could buy some of that," Penny began, but Dilys held up her hand.

"I must be off. I can't leave Pawl on his own for too long and I've got some hedgerows that need seeing to."

She nodded at Penny and then set off across the fields, the wind snatching at the hem of her overcoat.

Twenty-two

I want to go back and paint the cottages," Penny said to Gareth that evening. "Dilys seemed fine with it. Do you think I need to ask Mai?"

"I don't see why," Davies replied. "Dilys and Pawl apparently have the right to occupy the cottage, and you would be on the property with their permission so that seems in order."

"You know," said Penny, "there's something very strange going on with that property business. Gwennie took a phone call at Christmas—right here in my cottage—from Emyr telling her Ty Brith Hall had been sold. So was someone lying? Did Emyr lie about selling the property? Or was Mai lying about buying the property? I'm pretty sure she told Mrs. Lloyd and me that they had bought Ty Brith Hall, but now Dilys says they're renting it. That seems a strange kind of thing to lie about. I wonder why Mai wouldn't just say they're renting it?"

Davies shook his head. "I don't know. And maybe she doesn't know, either."

Penny gave him a sharp look. "What's that supposed to mean?"

"Well, there could be any number of reasons. Maybe Mai thinks they bought the property because that's what she was told, but her brother didn't actually buy it." He shrugged. "Or maybe he couldn't get the financing and was too embarrassed to tell the family. Maybe he changed his mind at the last minute. Maybe they have another property that hasn't sold. Or maybe, between the time Emyr told Gwennie the property had been sold and they actually took possession of the property, the deal fell through. It happens."

"Will you look into it?"

Davies considered the question.

"I don't think so. I can't see how the fact that they don't own Ty Brith could have any relevance to the murder of the daughter."

"You haven't mentioned the murder for a few days. Anything new there?" How's that coming along?"

"Not very well. Typically, you have evidence; you have witnesses. We don't have much of either, and we still haven't established a motive. The brother wasn't very helpful and the mother insisted on having a solicitor present when we interviewed the young lad, the brother, Tyler. He may know more than he's telling us. Or he may be protecting someone."

"Who?"

"Ah, well, if we knew the answer to that, we'd be much further on in the investigation."

"But if he's protecting someone, doesn't that mean . . . ?"

"Yes, it means it's a close-to-home murder. But we've known that from the beginning."

"How did you know that?"

"Because whoever killed her, knew her."

"How do you know that?"

"Because the extent of her injuries tell us that whoever killed her was close to her and killed her in a fit of rage. This wasn't a random killing."

"What do you think happened?"

Davies pinched his lips together.

"We have some holdbacks that we're not releasing because they're things only the killer could know. We want to save a few details that might be revealed in a confession." He pulled her closer to him. "And no, I'm not going to tell you what they are." He smiled at her. "Especially not you. Not this time. The less you know, the better. And you promised me you'd leave this case well alone, did you not?"

"Yes, I did," admitted Penny, adding to herself, but we didn't say anything about Victoria, did we?

He was just about to say something when loud, urgent knocking on the door startled them.

"You're not expecting anyone, are you?"

"No, I'm not. I wonder who it is."

"Well, there's only one way to find out. Shall I open it?"

Penny nodded. A moment later the rector burst through the door, his hat in his hand. "Oh, this is a bit of luck finding you both here." He was out of breath and paused for a moment to catch it.

"Shall I take your coat?" Penny asked, holding out her hand. He shook his head.

"No, I'm not staying. I've got to get home to Bronwyn, in case the kidnappers call."

"Kidnappers?" Davies looked startled.

"Dognappers. Our Robbie was taken this morning just before lunch. We rang you lot"—he gestured at Davies—"but the duty officer just said they'd take down the details and keep an eye out." He looked at Penny. "We want more than that, so Bronwyn suggested I should ask you to see if you could find him."

"I don't know what I could do," said Penny. "Of course, I want to help, but . . ."

"You've got to find him." The rector looked beseechingly from one to the other, his agitation and distress very close to the surface. "Bronwyn is that upset, she can't even drink a cup of tea. She blames herself, you see. She was busy with her newsletter so she let Robbie out into the garden on his own, and when she went out later, he was gone." He held up his hands. "Vanished."

He reached into his pocket and pulled out a couple of photographs. "I printed these off so you can show them around. We'll be putting posters up around the town tomorrow in case someone's found him."

Penny and Davies each accepted a photo. "I must get back. Bronwyn hasn't stopped crying all afternoon. It's terrible to see. I try to comfort her, but there's only one thing for it and that's to get Robbie home as quick as we can."

He looked from one to the other again, his kind face a mask of fear and grief.

"We'll do our best, Thomas," Davies said, placing a hand on his shoulder. "We'll do our best. You go home to Bronwyn now and leave it to us."

"That's the first time I ever heard you call him by his first name," Penny said when the rector had gone. "It sounded so right."

Twenty-three

It was heartbreaking," Penny said to Victoria the next morning. "I'm sure he was missing Robbie, too, but he was hurting so badly for his wife. And just before he arrived, I'd been feeling a bit hurt because Gareth isn't telling me everything he knows about Ashlee's murder. He knows things he's not telling me."

"Of course he knows things he's not telling you," Victoria replied. "He's the senior officer on a murder investigation."

"I know that, but I was a bit hurt when he wouldn't tell me the details of how Ashlee died."

"Hurt? Or put out? You saw real hurt and pain with the rector. Anyway, I'm sure Gareth has a very good reason. Or reasons," said Victoria as she turned to a spreadsheet on her computer. She pointed at the screen.

"Oh, there's something I wanted to mention to you. Most of the business is running really well. Hair, facials, massages are all bringing in what we projected. But the manicure salon"—she moved the cursor down a few lines, and then turned to face Penny—"takings are definitely down since the nail bar opened. It seems to be hurting our business. Can you think of anything we could do there to bring in more customers?"

"We're continuing to focus on our core group of customers, the more mature woman," Penny said stiffly. "And Eirlys is offering what she calls nail art to the younger set, and her friends can't get enough of it. The manicures take longer, but we can charge much more for them."

"Nail art?"

"She paints each nail to look like something—she's done that newspaper one, and the panda bears are utterly adorable! I had to order a dotting tool for that one, but it was well worth it. I challenged her to do a Burberry plaid, and it wouldn't surprise me if she actually did it."

"I wonder if we could charge more for her nail art and then give Eirlys a pay rise. We don't want to lose her and especially not to the competition."

"No," agreed Penny, "we certainly don't. But honestly, I don't think she'd go. Unless they offered her a lot more money, I suppose . . ." She shifted in her chair.

"Eirlys told me she's worried about her brother. He's suddenly got electronics and those fancy gadgets kids like these days and she's worried he's been stealing them."

"I know him," said Victoria, "and he's not that type of lad. He comes from a good family, as you very well know."

"Yes, but he might have fallen in with the wrong crowd," Penny pointed out. "Good kids do, sometimes, and they get led astray."

"Have you mentioned this to Gareth?"

"No."

"Why not?"

"Because he might feel he had to look into it, and I'd hate to get the boy in trouble."

"Well, there you go, then."

"What?"

"You don't see the connection between this and what he's doing?"

"No."

"He's not telling you the details of something he knows and you're doing the exact same thing."

Penny ran a hand over her chin. "I didn't think of it like that, but you might be right."

She lifted her coffee mug a few inches off Victoria's desk and then set it down again.

"There was something else. He warned me off the Ashlee Tran case, but he always tells me to stay away from the cases he's working on, so there's nothing new there. But there was something different about the way he said it this time." She sighed. "I don't know what I'm trying to say here. Of course he always means it, but it was as if this time he really means it, if you know what I mean."

She gave Victoria an anxious look. "So maybe you shouldn't go back up there. It could be dangerous."

"You're right, and anyway, it's turning out to be a waste of my time, although I did find it all very interesting, observing the family dynamics. When you're just a servant, you're a fly on the wall. Gwennie must have seen and heard so many things at the Hall all those years she worked there. So many secrets."

"She's very discreet, though. I don't think she's ever said a word about the Gruffydd family to me."

"Me, either."

"In the three or four times I was there I overheard some interesting things about the business, though. The mother is really distressed about her daughter's death and isn't going to work anymore. They've brought in a manager to run the nail and tanning place. Apparently, Derek, that's the husband, recommended her. The wife of his bookie, if you can believe it. It seems she spends more time on the tanning beds than any of the customers."

They both laughed.

"But I don't think they're a real or ongoing threat to our business, so at least we found that out. Oh, and another thing I heard is that they're growing strawberries. Maybe they're going to supply jam makers with berries."

"You mean they'll be growing strawberries this summer?"

"No, they grow them indoors."

"Well, that's interesting. Pawl Hughes mentioned something about expecting a gardener, so I guess that's what he meant."

"Who's Pawl Hughes when he's at home?"

"Oh, he used to be the head gardener up there at Ty Brith. He and his sister live in one of the tied cottages on the property."

Victoria closed the spreadsheet, took off her glasses, and rubbed her eyes.

"Anyway, all this talk's just reminded me where I left my umbrella. I think I'll just pop up to Ty Brith in the morning and pick it up, have a word with Mai, and that'll be the last time I go there. Hopefully, if I ever run into her in the street she won't recognize me without the pinny and scarf around my hair.

"Right, well, enough chat." She gestured at a couple of file folders on her desk. "You'd better get out of here so I can review these bids by lunchtime. I'm looking to see if we can generate more income by offering our own range of products or if we should stock well-known brands. I'll put some figures together and we can discuss later."

"Just make sure it all smells really, really expensive. And don't forget candles."

Penny paused in the doorway. "Oh, and there was something else I wanted to tell you. Dilys is in her seventies, but her hands look decades younger. She makes her own hand cream. I have no idea what's in it, but if we're going to offer our own line of products, that would be the one. Mrs. Lloyd mentioned something about our own branded line a while ago, and she might have been right. That hand cream would be brilliant.

"I thought I might go up to Ty Brith Hall in the morning to see Pawl and Dilys. We've got to have a sample of that hand cream. Why don't I pick up your umbrella while I'm there and I'll tell Mai you won't be returning."

"Oh, would you? That would be great." Victoria reached for her phone. "That frees up the morning for me to meet with these suppliers."

"And I think I'll take the rest of the day off to sketch up there," Penny said. "I wanted to paint the terraced cottages and the weather's meant to be good tomorrow, so I'll see you on Monday, then."

"Rhian, I'll be back in about ten minutes," Penny said as she passed the receptionist's desk a few minutes later. "Just popping out to the shops." Rhian looked up briefly, gave a little wave, and returned to her computer.

The weather had turned cold again, but the rain had held off for several days and the air felt wintry light and clean on Penny's face. The dry pavements had lured shoppers back onto the streets, and the town was bustling with mid-morning activity. She noticed a few customers in the Handz and Tanz, then turned the corner that led out of the town square onto a side street. She stopped as she always did to admire the window display in the bakery. She considered buying a few Eccles cakes to bring back to the Spa but decided to keep going. As she approached the butcher's, a small white dog tied up outside caught her attention and she stopped. The dog was watching the door of the butcher shop intently, waiting for its owner to return. Keeping the dog in her sights, she slipped into the doorway of a shop two doors down from the butcher and waited.

Across the street, a tall youth in a hoodie that partially obscured his face had also spotted the sitting dog. He waited for the traffic to clear and then, after looking in both directions, crossed the roadway. He reached the dog, and as he bent down to pat it, Penny recognized Eirlys's younger brother, Trefor. At that moment the dog's vigilance paid off, and a woman emerged from the butcher's carrying a shopping bag overflowing with parcels wrapped in brown paper. Wagging its tail in excited delight, the dog strained against its tether, trying to reach her.

Trefor stood up and walked quickly away, passing Penny just as the woman untied her dog and the two set off together in the opposite direction. Penny glanced after Trefor, but he had turned the corner into the town square. Her errand forgotten, she stepped out of the doorway and followed him, but by the

134

time she reached the square, just moments behind him, he was nowhere to be seen. Something about his behavior had seemed furtive, and she felt deep concern that Trefor was involved in the recent spate of dog thefts. That might account for his extra spending money. She wondered if she should have a word with Eirlys. But really, what could she say? That she'd seen Trefor patting a dog in the street? But what if she didn't say anything and another much-loved pet disappeared? A theft that might have been prevented if she'd told Gareth. Filled with doubt, she bent her head into the wind and returned to the Spa.

Twenty-four

In contrast to the bone-chilling cold outside, the heat and rain forest humidity inside the former stable block of Ty Brith Hall were almost unbearable. Thousands of small plants in square plastic containers sat on tables that stretched from one end of the long stone stable block to the other. Even the old box stalls, which used to be filled with warm, sweet-smelling hay, were crowded with small tables in which thousands of pots of germinating plants were laid out in symmetrical rows. Intensely bright overhead lights, connected by miles of electrical cables, threw long shadows against rough walls that dripped with condensation. A toned, shirtless Asian man walked slowly down the rows of tables, examining the distinctive light green, serrated leaves for signs of blight or infestation. He checked that the timers that controlled the lights were functioning properly so the plants would receive the correct amount of light for the right length of time. He made sure all the hoses that delivered water to the plants were open and flowing smoothly. Here he took a soil sample, there he took a measurement from a wall-mounted thermometer, entering his findings into a tablet.

At the end of the stable he slid open a green metal door that divided the stabling area from what had been the kennels, where generations of black Labrador dogs had been bred and whelped, and he entered the old kennel area.

Suddenly, he let out a roar, and reaching down, he pulled a youth off a low cot. He pulled a lit cigarette out of the boy's hand and stomped on it hard to extinguish it. Shouting at the boy, he punched him several times in the head, and when the boy crumpled to the stone floor, he kicked him in the back three or four times. The boy curled into himself as the man continued to beat him.

Finally, after delivering three or more heavy blows, panting heavily, he stopped.

Whimpering, the boy crawled back to his cot and burrowed into the filthy blankets. When the Asian man shouted at him again, he threw back the covers and scrabbled about in the pocket of his loosely fitting trousers, which resembled cotton pyjama bottoms, and handed over a cheap plastic cigarette lighter. Then he pulled the blankets over himself once more and turned his face to the wall.

Penny unlocked the back door of her cottage and stepped aside to let Trixxi enter. Like most dogs, Trixxi had her little idiosyncrasies, and one of them was that she always went through a door first. She pushed past Penny and dashed across the kitchen to her bowl beside the Rayburn in which Penny had placed a biscuit before they set off on their walk. Gwennie had left a long list of instructions on how to care for Trixxi, and Rule number 14 said that Trixxi should always find a treat in her bowl when she returned from a walk.

Penny put Trixxi's breakfast in her bowl, and leaving her to it, she went upstairs to get ready. About twenty minutes later, she put her coat back on and slipped a bottle of water into one pocket and a banana and cereal bar into the other. She had brought down a small manicure kit, and since there was no room in her outer coat pockets, she slid the manicure kit into an inner pocket of her coat. Eirlys had suggested they might want to stock a few kits in the Spa shop, and Victoria had obligingly ordered in a few samples. Depending on how things went when she stopped in to see Dilys and Pawl, Penny thought she might offer to look at Pawl's fingernails. On the table by the door she spotted a post-card that had been delivered the day before that she wanted to reread so on impulse she slipped it into an inner pocket. She clipped Trixxi's lead to her collar, and after locking the front door behind her, they set off together for the bus stop. On the way she reached into her pocket, and marveling that she hadn't lost one or both yet, she pulled on the blue angora woolen gloves Victoria had given her for Christmas.

Penny approached the back door of Ty Brith Hall, lifted the sliver dolphin knocker, and tapped three times. When there was no response, she tapped again. She took a step back and looked up at the windows. She saw no one, heard nothing, and sensed that unmistakably eerie, silent feel of a house with nobody home. She waited a few moments and then turned away, walking slowly with Trixxi in the direction of the stable. Once past it, they would pick up the footpath that led through the small wood to the terraced cottage where she expected to find Dilys and Pawl Hughes at home.

Built of grey stone, the two-storey stable formed a U-shape around a cobbled courtyard. Each stall had Dutch-style doors—top- and bottom-opening wooden doors that in the old days could have been opened from the inside or outside. With both halves open, the horse could be led directly into its stall from the courtyard without having to go through the stable proper. With the top open and bottom closed, the horse would have a good view of everything going on in the yard. Now, it looked as if someone had gone to a lot of trouble to bolt the doors shut and reinforce them with metal bars. In days gone by, the second floor of the building would have provided basic living accommodation for the grooms, with most of the space set aside for the storage of hay and straw.

As she reached the stable, Penny imagined the echoes of the gentle, rhythmic ring of metal horseshoes on cobbles as the horses were walked slowly into the courtyard after their morning ride, to be handed over to a waiting groom. Emyr Gruffydd's mother, the daughter of a blacksmith, had been a great rider; Penny had heard many stories from Mrs. Lloyd over the years on what a good seat she had, how much she had loved her animals, how well cared for they were, and how they always took first place at the annual agricultural fair.

Feeling the empty loneliness of the place, she wished she could have seen the stable yard when it had been bustling with grooms and riders and alive with the scent and sound of eager horses and excited dogs, anxious to be off on their morning run.

Instead, the space was quiet, forlorn, and the lack of life gave off a silent feeling of nothingness as if it were waiting for its chance to be useful again and fearing that day might never come.

In front of the last, heavily reinforced door, which opened into the building itself, and just before the smaller, lower addition that had been the Ty Brith kennels, she heard a faint scratching sound. She stopped and leaned against the door, listening. Probably just a rat, she told herself. They soon find empty buildings, and there's probably leftover bags of animal feed in the storerooms or even leather for them to chew in the tack room.

The scratching noise was followed by another sound, this time more like a thud, and louder. Trixxi waited, poised and alert, as Penny put her hand on the latch of the door and pressed it. She felt the mechanism lift on the other side and slowly pushed the door open. Blinded by the intensity of hundreds of powerful lights and assaulted by the unmistakable, pungent smell of marijuana, she gasped, covered her mouth, and stumbled backward, slipping off the low stone step. She twisted as she tried to straighten and then felt rough hands jerking her up by the arms.

"You shouldn't have done that, lady."

Twenty-five

"We'll just give those nails a moment to dry, Mrs. Jones."
Eirlys twisted the cap of the top-coat bottle closed and set it in the little basket on her treatment table, smiled at her customer, and stood up. "Excuse me a moment." She stepped out into the hall and, stifling a yawn, walked down the hall.

"This morning seems to be going really slowly, Rhian," she said. "Do I have one more customer or two before lunch?"

Rhian checked the bookings list on her computer. "One. And then you're to cover the desk while I go to lunch. I won't be long. Just want to get in a few things for the weekend." Eirlys nodded and returned to the manicure room. "All set, then, Mrs. Jones? Shall I help you on with your coat? Mind your nails, now. Sure you don't want a few minutes under the nail dryer?"

In her office, Victoria sighed and set down her coffee mug. She wasn't sure what she wanted for lunch. She clicked on her computer screen to minimize the document she was reading on and brought up the Internet. She'd heard about a music festival to be held in Florence in the spring, and she was curious to see if anyone she knew would be performing.

In Llandudno, Sergeant Bethan Morgan ducked her head into DCI Davies' office.

"I'm going to be leaving in a few minutes and just wondered if there's anything else you need me to do before I leave," she said. He looked up from his desk and smiled at her. "No, thanks, Bethan. Get yourself off and have a wonderful weekend."

"Got plans, sir?"

"I'm going to visit my son and his wife. I haven't seen them in ages, and I've got a feeling they want to tell me something. They've been asking me to come and see them for a few weeks and I really can't put it off. Although with everything that's going on"—he tapped the file on his desk—"this would probably be a better weekend to stay close to home."

He twirled his pen.

"Everything ready for Operation Sparrow? Everyone in place, as far as you know? Right, well, see you Sunday night, then. We'll meet here at seven P.M. sharp." She nodded, gave him an airy wave, and was gone. Davies returned to the Ashlee Tran file, searching for something he'd overlooked that could point him in the right direction.

He scrutinized the photos taken on the small hill where Ashlee's body had been found and then turned to the statement made by Ashlee's brother, Tyler. A few paragraphs in, his eyes narrowed and he leaned back in his chair and folded his arms. The boy's choice of words sent a message of smug confidence with a strong underpinning of evasiveness. Davies was struck by the coldness of his words. Every fibre in the policeman's body told him the boy knew something he was not telling. Something he knew was important but was withholding from them. But what? And why would he do that? Davies knew from long years of experience that lying by omission was as bad as, and sometimes worse than, outright deception. Both could send the investigation in the wrong direction, wasting precious time and resources.

Davies pushed himself away from his desk and stood up. He wandered over to the window and watched as menacing clouds assembled over the hilltops, hanging low and heavy in a dull, granite sky. He checked the time on his mobile. He still had to go home and pack for the overnight visit to his son's. He calculated the time it should take to drive there and wondered if he had enough time to stop off at Ty Brith Hall to talk to the lad, Tyler, who was now spending most of his time at the Hall with his family. No, better not. That conversation needed careful handling and they'd probably get better results if it was done in the more formal setting of a police interview room. He also wanted the interview videotaped so he could review the lad's body language.

He closed the file, slipped it into the top drawer of his desk, and shut down his computer. She was never far from his thoughts and as he pulled on his overcoat, he set aside the investigation and focused on Penny. He was wishing he'd had a chance to speak with her before he left and decided to ring her as soon as he got to his son's house. He realized he hadn't got her a gift for St. Dwynwen's Day; he'd think about that on the drive to Liverpool.

Twenty-six

Penny tried to wrench her arm from the strong grasp of the Asian man, but his grip was painfully tight. He pushed her into the short passageway between the stabling area and the kennels as she held tight to Trixxi's lead. Her heart sank as the heavy metal door clanged shut behind them.

"Who are you?" Penny demanded, pulling harder on her arm. "Let me go. You're hurting me." Unusual for a Labrador, known for their friendly, I-love-everybody natures, Trixxi let out a low, throaty growl and barked at him.

"Shut up, the pair of you." He pushed her along the passageway, crushing her arm as he maneuvered her in front of him along the uneven stone flooring, and then opening a wooden door, he pushed her into a small room. He grabbed her handbag by the shoulder strap and ripped it from her, then held his hand out for her other bag, which contained her art supplies. When she didn't move to hand it to him, he gestured to her with an impatient flap of his hand. He reached out, snatched it from her, and threw it into the corridor.

"Empty your pockets. Now."

She pulled out a bottle of water and the banana and cereal bar.

"You can keep."

With one last angry glare, he shut the door behind them and locked it.

With her heart pounding, she looked around in terrified disbelief. She was in what appeared to be the old tack room. Hooks at shoulder height all around the wood-paneled room, which had once held bridles, reins, and halters, were empty, as were the saddle racks beneath them. A small window set high up in the far wall let in feeble light filtered through cobwebs and dirt. The distinctive smell from the marijuana plants was less intense in here, but she knew that it was her knowledge of the plants, not the trespassing, that put her in grave danger. She told herself not to panic, to think things through, slowly and carefully. She unclipped Trixxi's lead, put her arms around her neck, and hugged her. She was glad Trixxi hadn't tried to attack the Asian man because if she had, Penny believed the man capable of killing her without a second thought.

A recent article in one of the Sunday papers had described in great detail the workings of a grow op—ordinary buildings turned into a nursery or hydroponics operation set up to grow marijuana plants and often owned by international criminal gangs. Private houses or commercial buildings were being converted into grow ops and they were becoming very popular because of their extreme profitability. The physical operations were dangerous. Because of the massive demand for electricity to run the lights and water to keep the plants hydrated, growers redirect the systems that bring these services into the property and tamper with the meters that measure consumption. The cost of the consumption is passed on to all consumers, and diverting electricity and tampering with electrical wiring, services usually performed by unqualified people, can lead to fires.

Re-venting the heating system to circulate air to feed the marijuana plants can circulate exhaust fumes from the furnace back into the building. Poisonous gases from the chemical nutrients used in the production of the crop can build up or have to be vented outside and released into the air.

And if all that weren't bad enough, the article said, these illegal operations bring criminals, weapons, and violence into what were once peaceful, law-abiding communities. A spokesman from the Royal Canadian Mounted Police quoted in the article said that in some areas of Canada, like British Columbia, one in eight homicides is related to the grow op industry.

Her hands began to shake. Now she was beginning to understand why Gareth had been so reluctant to discuss the newspaper story with her. Usually, when she showed an interest in a police matter in the news he was happy to explain it, offering an example or anecdote from his own experience or thoughtful insight into how he would handle it if it were his case and what the police whose case it was were likely doing. But this time he had looked slightly uncomfortable and said nothing. And then she remembered how he had warned her against coming here. A growing suspicion nibbled at the edges of her thought process. He knows, she thought. He knows about this grow op. He knows it's here and he knows what's going on. At that thought, she brightened. Was it likely that the police had the property under surveillance? If so, someone could have seen her being pushed against her will into this building. Perhaps at this very moment they were planning a daring raid to rescue her. But it had all happened so fast.

Did anyone know she was here? Victoria did, but she wasn't expecting to see her again until Monday. Gareth? He would be spending the weekend with his son and daughter-in-law in Liverpool. She looked at her watch. It was just after noon on Friday, and no one would be expecting to see her until Monday. If she lived that long.

She released her hold on Trixxi and rubbed Trixxi's head against her side. Then she walked over to a highly polished wooden trunk pushed against the back wall and lifted the lid, releasing a potent, dusty smell that seemed to combine hay with mud. A dark green cloth with the initials GG stitched in gold lay folded up inside the trunk. She pulled it out, and from its shape and the position of the straps and ties, she recognized it as a horse blanket. Initials GG. Gladwyn Gruffydd, Emyr's mother? Probably. Burrowing further into the box, she came across a smaller piece of material lined with sheepskin that she thought might be a saddle pad. She spread it on the floor as a bed for Trixxi. There didn't seem to be anything else in the trunk so she closed it and then sat on it. Beside the trunk was a metal bucket with a few bits of what she supposed were oats in the bottom.

There was little or no point, she thought, in banging on the door and demanding to be let out the way trapped women always seemed to do in films. There was no one to hear her—she knew that well enough. And even if, say, Dilys Hughes just happened to be walking by, how could she possibly hear Penny yelling for help through those impossibly thick stone walls?

The main thing was not to panic. She would have to think her way out of this.

At least it was warm here in the tack room, probably because of the intense lighting needed to run the massive grow op that had been set up throughout the building. So that's why this family was renting this property. A grow op was definitely not the sort of operation you'd expect to find in quiet, quaint North Wales and especially not Llanelen, with its gentle, prewar atmosphere. But the location was certainly secluded. No nosy neighbours to complain or poke their noses in when collectors arrived at all hours of the day and night to pick up product. No need to worry too much about security because no one ever came here.

And where there are drugs, there's money and lots of it, she reflected. So was the nail bar a front for money laundering? Probably. It was all starting to make sense now. That was why Mai didn't care whether the business was profitable or not. It didn't need to be. The drugs money was run through the nail bar's books and came out the other side on its way to an offshore account. And Mai, what was her role in all this? Was she in on the scheme? Difficult to see how she couldn't be. If she ran the nail bar and tanning salon she had to know what the accounts looked like. Or did she? Penny thought about her involvement at the Llanelen Spa. As the general manager, Victoria was responsible for the operations and she looked after the accounts. If she was fiddling the books, would Penny know? Maybe not.

Trixxi got up and went to the door, looked back at Penny, and wagged her tail.

"You need to go out, girl." Penny walked over to the door

and banged on it. "Hey," she yelled, "my dog needs to go out. Let us out of here." Trixxi made little whining noises and then returned to the saddle blanket and sat down, fixing her trusting brown eyes on Penny's face.

I'll need to go myself before long. She thought of the bucket and hoped it wouldn't come to that.

She eyed the window. Even if she could somehow get the window open, she'd never be able to lift Trixxi through it, and she couldn't, wouldn't leave Trixxi behind.

She returned to the door and bent down to look through the keyhole, but could see nothing because something was blocking her view. If the key was in the lock, she couldn't believe her luck.

Looking closer at the lock, she realized it was one of those surprisingly solid mechanisms that used an old-fashioned skeleton key with a long cylindrical shaft and a single, minimal flat, rectangular tooth or bit. People often kept the key in the lock and just turned it to lock or unlock the door, as needed. This type of key could unlock the mechanism from either side of the door, and she'd seen on a television program once how to get the key from the outside to the inside. You just needed a piece of paper and something fairly long and thin, like the refill from a ballpoint pen. Unfortunately, the Asian man had taken away her bag of sketching materials, which contained both.

She looked around the room. There was nothing that would slide under the door for the key to land on, but there might be something in the manicure kit in her coat pocket that she could use to push the key out of the lock.

She felt in her coat pocket and pulled out the postcard. She looked at the photo of Wells Cathedral and turned it over to read the message written in the distinctive, careful handwriting of a former schoolteacher, her new friend Dorothy Martin. It was a start, but it wouldn't provide enough landing area when she pushed the key out of its hole. But she thought she could combine it with one of the plastic dog bags she always carried with her. She pulled one out of her trouser pocket and tore it apart to create a bigger area and set the postcard on top of it. Then, kneeling and bending over, she laid the small green bag out flat, patted the card down on top of it, and gently pushed them underneath the door beneath the lock. She straightened up and, with the lock at eye level, poked at the key with the cuticle tool from the manicure kit until it fell, making a tinkling sound as it hit the stone floor on the other side of the door. A tiny bit of daylight filled the keyhole.

Muttering a prayer that the key had not bounced off the dog bag when it landed, she bent down again and slowly pulled the bag back under the door. And there it was . . . the key. She picked it up, inserted it into the keyhole, and turned it. She felt the tension on the lock as the key tightened its grip on the lock and slowly pulled the bolt into the door.

She turned to Trixxi and gestured to her to come. Trixxi obediently stood, wagged her tail, and joined Penny at the door. Penny clipped her lead on her.

As quietly as she could, Penny turned the door handle and opened the door a few inches. She listened, and when she heard nothing, she opened the door a little bit wider. When she judged it was open just wide enough, she stood aside to let Trixxi go through and then followed her into the corridor. Ahead of her was the door that led to the outside, to her left the kennel area, and on her right the narrow corridor led deeper into the stable, past the old stalls, now filled with thousands of budding marijuana plants in various stages of growth.

Suddenly, from her left she heard a quick movement, and a moment later a short Asian boy stood in front of her, blocking her way to the door and the freedom beyond.

"Who are you? What are you doing here?" she asked softly as she prepared to put her hand on his shoulder and brush him aside so she could get to the door.

"Trung," he said, pointing to himself. "You got food for me?"

She reached into her coat pocket for the cereal bar, and then, just as she handed it to him, an angry shout from farther down the passageway made her heart sink.

She brushed past the boy and lunged for the door. She managed to get her hand on the door handle and tried to turn it. It didn't move. She dropped her clammy hand, and by the time the Asian man who had locked her in the tack room reached her, her heart was beating so wildly she thought it would surely burst. She opened her mouth to speak, but her mouth was so dry and she was breathing so hard she couldn't form the words. With the fear in her stomach now a hard knot of pain, she looked around frantically to see if there was somewhere to run. The Asian man, his dark brown eyes cold and glittering, was blocking the way down the long passage, the door to the outside was locked, behind her was the tack room she had just escaped from, and to her left was the door that led to the former kennel. She pushed the boy out of the way and bolted through the doorway that led to the kennels, hoping to find an unlocked door that would lead to the outside, knowing as she did so that her chance of outrunning the Asian man was slim to none. But every fibre in her adrenaline-fueled body told her she had to try.

Twenty-seven

*D*avies pressed the button to end the call and then stared at his phone as if willing it to tell him something. Unable to reach Penny all afternoon, he'd left a couple of messages asking her to ring him back, but as time passed and he didn't hear from her, he was beginning to worry. He hadn't spoken to her since last night, and now that afternoon had given way to evening, he was becoming increasingly unsettled

"Dad! Dinner's ready." His son calling up the stairs interrupted his thoughts. He considered his black suitcase sitting on the floor waiting to be unpacked and then glanced around the small bedroom. Owen and Hillary wanted to tell him something over dinner, and he had a pretty good idea what it was. He hated the thought of ruining their moment. The clock on the bedside table said seven o'clock. He got up off the bed, his mind made up. He'd have dinner, then ring her one more time. If he couldn't reach her, even though he knew his son wouldn't like it, he'd make his apologies and return home.

"Coming," he called. "Be right down."

He scrolled through his directory until he found the number he needed and then pressed SEND. A moment later his call was answered.

"Ah, Victoria, hello, it's Gareth here. Glad I caught you. How are you?"

He listened for a moment.

"Good, good. Well, listen, it's actually Penny I'm ringing you about. I haven't heard from her today and can't reach her. She's not answering her phone and I'm getting a little worried. Have you heard from her? Do you know where she is? Is everything all right?"

Davies rubbed his chin as Victoria explained she'd spoken to Penny earlier in the day and thought she'd gone to Ty Brith Hall to sketch some outbuildings.

"Well, listen. I'm at my son's in Liverpool so I need you to go round to Penny's. You've got a key, yes? Right, well go in and see if she's there. If not"—he thought for a moment—"text me and let me know. I'll come back, if need be. I'll wait to hear from you, but you must get back to me as quickly as you can."

He rang off, put his phone in his pocket, and went downstairs.

Hillary had gone to some trouble. With both of them working long hours as solicitors, they didn't have a lot of time for entertaining. When they got together with friends, it was over a takeaway pizza or at a trendy restaurant in town. Like most young couples, they did not have a formal dining room, so the table in their large, modern kitchen had been set with a pink cloth and a bouquet of pink roses, their stems trimmed short, had been carefully arranged in a glass bowl and set in the middle of the table. There's a clue, he thought. With her hand encased in an oven mitt, Hillary pointed him to a chair as Owen poured two glasses of wine, one for himself and one for Davies. He filled a third glass with sparkling mineral water. There's another clue, thought Davies.

Hillary set a large aluminum pan of steaming supermarket lasagna on the table and then turned back to the counter to get a loaf of French bread. At the sight of the bread, Davies' stomach clenched. Penny loved bread and he remembered her telling him once how she used to enjoy baking it. His hand folded around his mobile, willing it to ring.

Owen raised his glass of wine, Hillary picked up her glass of sparkling mineral water, and they smiled into each other's eyes.

"Well, Dad," said Owen as Davies reached for his glass of wine, "cheers. We've really been looking forward to your visit because we wanted to tell you something in person." He reached for Hillary's hand. "We're going to have a baby. Hill's about three months along. We don't know yet if it's a boy or girl"—he gestured at the table—"but we went with pink."

"That's great news." Davies smiled at them. "I'm really happy for you both. Congratulations. I know you'll be wonderful parents."

"Well," said Hillary, slicing the bread, "tuck in before it gets cold. Owen, pass your dad the salad."

Davies set down his wineglass, untouched. "Sorry, son, there's something going on that's got me worried. I'll have to make some calls after dinner, and depending on what happens, I'm afraid I may have to head back to Wales tonight." He caught the disappointed look tinged with anger that flashed across his son's face. "I'm truly sorry, Owen. I'd been looking forward to spending the weekend with you, I want you to know that."

Owen turned to his wife. "It was like this when we were growing up. He always put the work first, family second."

"It's not like that, Owen," Davies said gently. "A friend of mine, a lady I care about very much . . ." His voice trailed off. "She went out today to do some sketching and I can't reach her on her mobile."

"So her phone's switched off. Or maybe she's in one of those places where there's no reception. There are dead spots in the valley. It's not a big deal. Don't worry about it."

"I've been a copper for a long time, and I know when something's not right. I know when to trust my instinct, and this is one of those times." Davies' phone buzzed and he stood up. "Excuse me." He stepped away from the table and read Victoria's text. *Not here. No Trixxi. Nothing looks disturbed.* Davies rang Penny's phone. As soon as he heard her voice mail he ended the call, knowing what he had to do.

"I'm sorry, Owen," he apologized again. "I've got to go. I'll just get my things." As he walked toward the stairs Owen muttered, "I knew this would happen. He never changes."

"Don't be so hard on him," said Hillary as she cut a serving of lasagna and set it on her husband's plate. "This isn't work, it's personal. Can't you see how worked up he is? The poor man's practically beside himself with worry. Let him go."

Davies shut the car door and started the motor. He sat there for a few moments, thinking, and then reached for his mobile and placed a call. When Bethan Morgan picked up, he got right to the point.

"Bethan, we've got trouble. It's Penny. I think she's up there at Ty Brith and these are not warm, friendly people. If they do have her, we've got to get her out in case things get nasty. Let's hope we're not too late.

"We're going to have to move up Operation Sparrow and launch it tonight. Can you notify the CMU team and get everyone in position? I'm leaving now and should be back in two hours or so." He listened. "I know, and I'm sorry. That's 2130 hours for the briefing." Bethan asked a few more questions and he replied, "No, we don't need a search warrant for the Penny part of this. I have reason to believe that someone is in danger at that location, and that gives us the right to enter and search the property. But we'll need one to take the computers from the house and we need to make sure we get every last one of them." He rang off, put the car in gear, and drove into the night.

Twenty-eight

Penny sat blindfolded on the floor, her knees pulled up to her chest and her arms tied behind her back. The steel door that led from the kennel to the freedom of the stable court-yard was locked, and in seconds the Asian man had her once again in his grip. She'd tried to shake him off, but he had over-powered her as the Asian boy watched and another man came running. One of the men had given Trixxi to the boy, and then together they propelled Penny toward the house. When they got close to the back door, the first man said something to the other one and he produced a piece of black cloth that they tied over Penny's eyes. They then bound her hands before jostling her over the threshold. She tried to remember which way they were going but after a few turns she was completely disoriented. She did note, though, that they had not gone up or down any stairs. Then she was pushed into what felt to her like a confined space, and the door was shut firmly behind her. She backed up until she could feel the door handle and tried to turn it. Of course, it was locked.

The room smelled as if it had been recently cleaned by someone with a heavy hand. There was a sharp and unpleasantly overpowering odor. Was it bleach? Some kind of industrial disinfectant, she thought. Beneath her feet she felt carpet, and slowly she sank down until she was sitting on the floor. A few moments later she heard the door open. Even more frightened and with her pulse pounding, she turned her face to the sound.

"Who is it?" she croaked.

The person said nothing but reached down and removed the tie from her hands, waited while she brought her hands around to the front of her body, and then placed a mug of hot tea in them. As he bent over her, Penny caught a strong smell of stale cigarette smoke. The door then closed with a metallic click and Penny was once more alone. Her hands were trembling so much she was afraid she would spill the contents before she could set the mug down, but somehow she managed to do it. She rubbed her hands together, then reached up and lifted the blindfold.

She was in a small, windowless, irregularly shaped room that seemed to be some kind of storage area. Metal shelving along one wall held nothing but a laptop computer. A single, dim bulb burned overhead, casting long shadows against the wall. A rectangular, heavily patterned burgundy carpet had been placed over a hardwood floor stained a dark brown. She crawled across the carpet and leaned against the far wall, legs outstretched in front of her, facing the door. She ran her hand over the carpet; it felt smooth and clean. She sniffed the air again. What was that awful smell?

Shaking with fear and trying not to panic, she wrapped her hands around the mug of tea, drawing comfort from its soothing, homey warmth. She took a sip. It was strong and sweet. She looked at the mug while she tried to organize her thoughts. Who had brought it to her? Why? Her mouth was unbearably dry and she was desperate for something to drink. She raised the cup to her lips again, then stopped. What if it was poisoned or had been laced with something to knock her out? She set it down beside her, then pushed it back behind her, against the wall. She didn't want it to spill and it might come in handy later.

What have they done with Trixxi? she wondered. At the thought of the gentle, loving dog being hurt or worse, a wave of sadness washed over her and her eyes filled with tears. She pictured Trixxi rambling cheerfully along the country lanes, nose to the ground, tail wagging, discovering something new and wonderful every few steps. She loved the feel of Trixxi's glossy black fur and the way she looked at her with those trusting, adoring brown eyes.

She sighed, wiped her eyes, and then, to her surprise, yawned. What was she supposed to do now? Wait, she guessed, for something to happen. Someone would have to come for her sooner or later. They wouldn't just abandon her here, would they?

That thought sent a cold shiver of terror through her. What if the people who lived here, Mai and her husband and everybody else, had just packed up and gone back to Birmingham, leaving her here to die of thirst or starve to death?

Or maybe she was just being held here while they decided what to do with her. She licked her lips and tried to swallow. No, she would not let them determine her fate, and the thought of Trixxi strengthened her resolve. She would get out of here or die trying. She would not make it easy for them. Think, Penny, she told herself. Think.

At least her hands were free now, and there was a light in the room. She thought about the door and what kind of lock it might have. She patted her pockets. She discovered she'd left the little manicure kit behind in the stable so she had no tools to pick the lock, even if she had known how, and anyway, those little tools would be useless against a lock like this one. She thought about how it had sounded when it locked. Metallic and sharp, not clunky and slow, as it would with a manual key.

She had never heard Gwennie mention this room and wondered if it had been added since the Vietnamese people had taken over the house. The room might have existed when the Gruffydd family lived here, she decided, but perhaps the new occupants had installed a more modern locking system.

She stood up and, trailing a hand against the wall, walked around the small room, exploring and feeling the wall as she went. The walls were bare and the room contained next to nothing, just the carpet and a rack of metal shelving holding a laptop. Shelving, carpet, and a laptop. Since that was all there was, she would explore every inch of them, starting with the laptop.

Doubting that Wi-Fi would work in this enclosed, windowless room, she opened the lid. Password required. She halfheartedly tried entering a few . . . Ashlee, Ashlee1, Tyler, Ashty. Nothing. The password would probably be a Vietnamese word. She replaced the laptop on the shelf and turned her attention to the carpet.

She took off her boots and placed them neatly side by side near the door and walked back to the carpet. She ran her feet along the nap, seeing if anything would come up. Nothing did. But the colour looked refreshed, as if it had been recently cleaned. Why, she asked herself, why would someone bother to wash the carpet in a storage room? She lifted up the two corners of the carpet nearest the door and saw nothing. She did the same with the third corner and saw nothing. As she lifted the fourth corner, the carpet gave up its secret, revealing a glint of something shoved between the floorboards. She lay down on her stomach to get a closer look, and as she reached out to try to pry it loose, she stopped, her hand in midair. Don't touch it, she told herself, it might be evidence. It was a dangly type of earring with a silver hook and a small purple stone, and she realized where she had seen it before. Gareth had shown one just like it to her and Alwynne; it was the mate to the one found on Ashlee's body.

I wonder if poor Ashlee was held in this room, too, and she jammed the earring between the floorboards to let us know she was here, Penny thought. Clever girl. But if she'd been here, locked up in this room, did that mean . . .

With her next breath the antiseptic smell, which she'd been getting used to, seemed overpowering again and her heart banged against her ribs with such force she could feel its every wringing motion. A hard knot of fear tightened in her gut. The disinfectant smell nauseated her. She pushed the back of her hand against her mouth to stifle a scream.

Had Ashlee screamed, she wondered, when she'd been beaten to death? In this room.

Twenty-nine

I just hope we're not too late."

"So do I," said Sergeant Bethan Morgan. "If she's there, that is. Because you don't know for sure that she is, do you? She might have gone sketching with Trixxi and then met up with a friend and stayed for dinner. She could have done any number of things. Be any number of places."

The two officers were in the lead car of a small convoy winding its way out of Llanelen and up the road that led to Ty Brith Hall. The last time they had driven that route was to advise Mai Grimstead to prepare herself to face the reality that the body Penny had discovered on the hillside was that of her daughter, Ashlee.

Davies grimaced and shifted in his seat. "When you've been a police officer as long as I have, Bethan, you just know when something is very wrong. And this is very wrong. We can't take the chance that she's okay somewhere and that she'll just turn up wondering what all the fuss is about."

Bethan, who was driving, stole a sideways glance to her left at Davies in the passenger seat. He had a binder on his lap and with a pinpoint flashlight was reviewing his operational notes.

"Now we have the CMU team ready to take the stables and secure the grow op. You'll stay with me but keep in touch with Jones, who'll be leading the team in the house. We want a full and thorough search. Attics, basements, everything. Hopefully we find her, but if not, look for anything that might indicate she was there."

Bethan nodded. "I was wondering, sir, if you mentioned the grow op to Penny. Did she know about it?"

"Really, Sergeant, I'm surprised you'd even ask such a thing. Of course I didn't tell her about it. Not only would that be highly unprofessional, but with an operation as sensitive and expensive as this one, putting it at risk would be the last thing I'd do."

"I didn't mean it that way, sir. Quite the opposite, in fact. I was thinking about her safety. You know how she always winds up getting involved somehow in our murder cases—despite our best efforts to keep her out. So I was thinking she might have stumbled into something really bad up here whilst trying to investigate Ashlee's murder. When, in fact, if you'd told her what was really going on at Ty Brith—the grow op—she would have known to keep well away."

"Oh, bloody hell, Bethan, I never thought of it that way. I was just doing everything by the book, which of course means tell no one. But you may be right. It might have been better if she'd known."

Bethan flipped on the turn indicator, then slowed, easing the car onto the road that led to the Hall, as Davies glanced in the wing mirror at the cars following. Their headlights were on, but there were no flashing blue lights or sirens. As the vehicles reached the top of the road that led to the Hall, the convoy divided as some cars, led by Davies and Bethan, turned right toward the stables, leaving the last two cars to turn left toward the house.

"What've you done now, Derek?" sneered Tyler as they watched the two cars approach. "Fallen behind in your payments to the bookies, have ya?"

Derek let the curtain fall from his hand and turned to his stepson. "Here comes trouble. Big-time. It's the police. Where's your mother?"

Tyler shrugged. "I think she's outside somewhere talking to Uncle Tu'."

"What about Bruno? Is he with them?"

"How should I know? Oh, no, wait a minute. I think I heard Uncle Tu' say he's looking after something in Birmingham and he's expected back Sunday."

"Well, you'd better go and see if you can find your mother. She's—" He was interrupted by a loud banging on the front door accompanied by shouts of "Open up! Police!"

Derek inclined his head toward the door. "It may be too late."

By now the seriousness of the situation was dawning on Tyler. "But do we have to let them in? What do they want? Don't they need a search warrant or something?"

"If they need one, they've got one. They know how these

169

things work and they tend to come prepared." The knocking continued. "Better let 'em in. They're coming in anyway, so we might as well spare them the bother of having to break the door down."

Derek walked toward the door, shouting as he went, "All right! Hold your horses. I'm coming."

A moment later, Derek led PC Chris Jones from the Conwy station into the spacious reception room at the front of the house.

"We're looking for a woman called Penny Brannigan," Jones said, holding up his official identification, "and we have reasonable grounds to believe she may be in this house. Do you know anything about her?"

Derek shook his head. "No, I don't know anything about her. Do you, Tyler?"

Tyler shook his head. "Who's she, when she's at home?"

"Well, you won't mind if we search the house, then, will you, sir?"

"Have you got a search warrant?" Tyler asked.

"Yes, although we don't need one. We have reason to believe that a crime is being committed here and someone's in danger, and that gives us the right of entry."

Derek's shoulders sagged as Jones returned to the front hall where several officers stood waiting. He nodded at them and they spread out through the building.

"Mind you don't break anything, now, lads," Derek called after them.

He turned to Tyler. "What if they find . . . ?" Tyler said in a low voice.

Derek shook his head. "They won't."

Thirty

*B*ethan Morgan ended the phone call and, shaking her head, turned to Davies. "They've finished the house search. Sorry, but they didn't find any trace of Penny."

Davies ran his hand over his upper lip. "Did they do the cellar and attic?" Bethan nodded.

"But, sir, I've had an idea. These old houses often have hiding places, secret rooms, priest holes, that sort of thing. Our team won't be able to find them because they weren't meant to be found. If anyone would know, Gwennie would. She was the housekeeper here for years."

"Ring her. Victoria can give you her number. Tell Jones to stay where he is until he hears from you."

A few moments later, Bethan nodded excitedly and turned to Davies. "There is one. It's off the butler's pantry between the kitchen and dining room."

"Call Jones."

Jones pressed the END button on his phone and turned to Derek.

"All right now, mate, there's one more room we'd like to search. I think you know which one I mean. Show me where it is."

Derek led Jones into the kitchen and then into a large butler's pantry, situated between the kitchen and dining room. The walls were lined with bespoke cabinets, mostly empty, but at one time they would have held silver and crockery in a heavy, old-fashioned pattern. A small desk in one corner would have held the wine journal and other records of the day-to-day operation of a large household. The wide oak floorboards creaked under the men's weight. Derek approached one of the cabinets and reached under the middle shelf. The cabinet then slowly swung toward them, revealing a solid door behind it. As the police officers exchanged glances, a mechanical bolt slid back with a loud click and Derek pushed the door open. He stepped to one side so the police officers could enter. The room was empty. Jones bent over and picked up a blue woolen glove.

"She wasn't there?" said Davies. "How can that be? We've looked everywhere, but she's here, somewhere. I know she is." And then, more to himself, he added, "She's got to be."

Jones showed him the glove. "Is this hers?" Davies took it from him and, turning it over, he nodded. "We found that in the secret room. She must have left it behind to let us know she was there. Maybe they've taken her somewhere else. I hope not, but they could have moved her on."

They were silent for a moment as a sudden burst of crackle over their radios drowned out any other sound.

"We've got the husband and son who were in the house waiting in the back of a car. Is there anything else you need us to do in here?" Jones asked.

"Not at the moment," said Davies. He was about to add something when a voice came over the loud-hailer. "Stand clear."

The officers took a few steps back, and several seconds later a huge explosion ripped through the stable. Large pieces of metal debris fell through the smoke, followed by loud, ringing clangs as they made contact with the cobbled yard. As the smoke cleared, revealing the extent of the damage, a disembodied voice shouted, "You were only supposed to blow the bloody doors off."

As great shouts of tension-releasing laughter went up, a shadowy figure emerged from around the far side of the building. Jones spotted it first, tapped Davies on the arm, and pointed.

Ignoring the CMU's warning to keep back, Davies ran toward Penny. He had just wrapped his arms around her when an intense humming sound, followed by a loud crackling, hissing noise, came from within the building. Seconds later, staccato bursts of high-voltage sparking signaled that the electrical wiring was about to reach the end of its vastly overloaded capacity.

"Here we go, everybody," shouted the CMU commander. "Keep back and clear the way for the fire brigade."

Thirty-one

*A*fter one more loud crack and a series of small explosions, smoke began billowing out of the hole in the side of the stable building where the reinforced steel door had been. A moment later, a boy stumbled out, coughing and covering his mouth.

"That's Trung," shouted Penny. As two paramedics went to help him, the boy began yelling and pointing at the kennels.

"Oh, my God, there must be dogs trapped in there," Penny shouted. "Trixxi might be in there." She grabbed Davies' arm. "Do something! You've got to get them out."

"Wait here," he said. "Don't move. I'll tell the CMU commander." He ran a few steps and then turned back to make sure Penny had not moved. He raised an arm toward her. "Stay where you are."

Penny ran up to him.

"You can access the kennels through an interior door. They'll be on the right if you go in through that hole you blew open.

Tell them that." She grabbed his arm. "Believe me, I've had more than enough for one day. I'm not going anywhere." She took a few steps backward, her arms clutched in front of her.

Davies exchanged a few words with the CMU commander, who dispatched a couple of his officers. Soon, loud frantic barking could be heard as a couple of officers staggered from the smoking building. One had his hands full with four dogs on leads, and another had an armful of wriggling fur that might have been two or three dogs.

Penny ran up to the officer with the dogs on leads. "That Lab," she said, "is mine." She bent down and wrapped her arms around Trixxi, who wagged her tail vigorously, and her whole back end with it, as she buried her face in Penny's arms. With tears streaking down her face, Penny stood up slowly, adjusting the blanket that a medic had placed around her shoulders.

Davies put his arm around her and waved over his sergeant, Bethan Morgan.

"Look, Penny," he said, "I need you and Trixxi to wait in a nice, warm police car with Bethan. You'll need to give us a statement, and if you feel like talking, Bethan can take it now. If you want to wait until tomorrow, that's fine, too." Bethan slipped her hand through Penny's arm, and giving her a concerned but determined look, she led her to the staging area where the police cars had been parked.

"We're just rounding everyone up now," said Bethan, "and trying to sort all this out. It's going to take a bit of time, but I could drive you home if you like."

Penny shook her head.

"I think I'd rather wait and go home later. I don't really want to be alone right now."

"Of course you don't. But it's getting late and you've been through a lot. If you do want to go home, I'll check if it's okay with him if I stay with you." She gave Penny a knowing smile. "I'm sure it will be fine with him, if that's what you want. They can spare me and he'll want what's best for you."

Penny reached inside her coat and pulled out a laptop. "Here, take this," she said, handing it to Bethan. "I found it in the small room where they held me. I figured you'd want it. It seems it was important enough to be the only thing they kept under lock and key. And that room, you'll want to get the forensics team to give it a good going-over. I've got an awful feeling something really bad happened in there."

As they reached the car, an explosion from behind made them turn around. They watched in horror as a shower of sparks flew up and the loud crackling of licking flames signaled that the stable was now fully engulfed.

Then, above the roar of the fire they heard a police officer shouting. Penny and Bethan looked at each other.

"What did he say?" Bethan asked. "I didn't catch what he said." Penny grabbed the young police officer's arm. "It sounded like, 'Get back. You can't go in there.'"

The commotion at the stables and the bright orange light wavering over the treetops had awakened Pawl and Dilys Hughes. Tying the sash of her dressing gown around her waist as she entered Pawl's bedroom, Dilys tried to soothe him. "Now, Pawl, it'll just be something happening up at the Hall, but it's nothing to do with us. We're all right here. You go back to sleep now."

Pawl moaned and lay back against his pillow as Dilys closed

the door quietly and returned to her room. An eerie, uneven light began to seep through the window, casting flickering shadows on the wall, and lapping at his bed like an orange-red sea. Frightened, he climbed out of bed and shuffled over to the window. A warm, iridescent glow bathed the contours of his face as he looked toward the source of the light. Clearly visible through the black, skeletal tree branches, angry flames shot through the roof of the stable, lighting up the night sky and filling the air with dense, black smoke that was obliterating what had been a canopy of bright stars on a clear, frosty night. He let out an anguished cry that sounded as if it came from a terrified, wounded animal. Grasping the furniture to steady himself, he made for the door.

"Who just went in there?" demanded Davies. "Everyone had been ordered to keep back. What the hell's going on here?" He turned to the fire brigade's senior divisional officer, who was managing the firefighting efforts.

"I don't know who he is or how he got past us." The emergency radio crackled as he contacted the firefighters in the building. He listened for a moment and then turned to Davies. "He ran into the old kennel part shouting something. They're trying to get him out, but he's resisting."

They turned to a distraught woman shivering in a dressing gown.

"That's my brother, Pawl," she cried. "I tried to stop him, but I couldn't. He just ran in there. Oh, dear God." She bent over, breathing hard.

"The firefighters are trying to get him out," Davies told her.

"Whatever would have possessed him to run into a building that's on fire?"

"He's got dementia and he's confused. He's living in the past. He used to be in love with the kennel maid here and he probably thinks she's in there and the poor old fool rushed in to try to save her." She covered her face with her hands and started to cry. "Look," said Davies, "the firefighters are doing everything they can. I expect they'll be bringing him out in a moment." Davies motioned to a woman police officer. "Get her a blanket and take care of her," he said in a low voice.

The intense heat from the fire drove the little group back. Their faces reflected the bright light of the fire as a group of firefighters emerged from the building, their heavy equipment forcing them to walk slowly and awkwardly. They carried a large bundle, which they set down on the ground. One of them waved to the paramedics, who rushed over. Dilys started forward, but Davies put a restraining hand on her arm and shook his head.

"Let them do their work," he said, as a paramedic bent over the still figure.

And then the paramedic turned and gestured to someone, who brought a blanket to cover Pawl's body.

Thirty-two

"How are you feeling?" Victoria asked the next morning.

"Not too bad, I guess, all things considered," said Penny. "It could have been much, much worse, I know that." She took a sip of coffee and set her cup down. "I didn't sleep very well, though. I would just be drifting off, finally, and then I'd be right back there. It was so vivid. My heart would be pounding and I'd feel the same emotions I felt at the time, in a very real way." Before Victoria could say anything, Gwennie, who had arrived at the cottage unannounced and started cooking breakfast, approached the table, offering a boiled egg and toast. Penny shook her head, but Gwennie set the plate down in front of her anyway.

"Come on now, you've got to keep your strength up, Miss Penny."

Penny smiled up at her. "Why do people always say that, I wonder."

Victoria waited until Gwennie returned to the kitchen. "Because there's some truth in it? And it makes other people feel better. Sorting out a cup of tea or whatever gives them something to do. Lets them feel useful."

Penny gazed at the lightly speckled brown egg Gwennie had placed in front of her, and Victoria gestured at it. "Go on. Gwennie's watching and it will make her feel better if you eat a bit of it. She came over here specially because she wanted to try to make you feel better. This is her way of showing you that she cares about you."

"I didn't think of it like that," said Penny, "but you're right." She smiled at Gwennie and began tapping the top of the egg with the back of a spoon. "Just eat what you can," said Victoria, "and then we'll give the rest to Trixxi." At the mention of her name, Trixxi looked up hopefully from her basket beside the Rayburn and thumped her tail.

Penny nibbled at the edge of a piece of toast, which Gwennie had cut into soldiers, strips perfect for dunking into the runny egg yolk. Victoria took a sip of coffee. The silence stretched on until Victoria finally said, "Well, you know we're dying to hear what happened. Do you feel up to telling us?"

"Us?"

"Well, Gwennie and me." Victoria tilted her head toward the kitchen. Gwennie set her cloth down, put her hand in her apron pocket, and took a few steps toward the table.

"The lady police officer, Bethan, she called me last night at my sister's, asking if there was a secret room up at the Hall. I told her where it was and she said they'd send the police there to find you. I told them how to unlock the door." Gwennie nodded. "So I was glad they found you and were able to get you out."

"They didn't get me out, though, Gwennie. I figured it out for myself."

A wide smile spread across Gwennie's face.

"Did you now, Miss Penny! Good for you."

Victoria looked confused and she glanced from one to the other. "What? Tell me what happened."

"They locked me in this little room, which I found out later was just off the kitchen. When the door locked, the mechanism sounded mechanical or automatic, not something that used a key. I wasn't sure if the room had been in use when the Gruffydd family lived there or if the Vietnamese people had had it installed, but I thought it probable that it was the result of that major renovation done in, oh, when was it, Gwennie? Mrs. Lloyd told me that Emyr's mother and father had the place all done up in the 1960s, I think."

"That's right, but they had the kitchen done again about twenty years later. Nothing goes out of style faster than a kitchen."

"Right, so anyway, I sat there for a while and thought about it, and I figured that if the room had been installed when Emyr was a boy, his mother would have put in a way for him to get out if he was ever locked in. So I realized that the button to unlock the door would be low, child height, so he could reach it."

"Good for you," Gwennie said again. "Good thinking I call that."

"So I looked around the room, low, for something unusual, and behind the shelves at one end, I found what looked like a push-button light switch. I thought it might be a panic button. If it was pressed, a bell would ring somewhere in the house to set off an alarm that someone was locked in that room. But anyway, I pushed the button, the lock clicked, the door slid open,

183

and believe me, I didn't waste any time getting the hell out of there. I realized pretty quickly I was near the kitchen so I got out by the back door and was heading around behind the stables, and then I saw the fire and everything else going on. I thought the safest thing to do would be to head toward the firefighters, but the police were there, too, so at that point I knew I was safe." She looked from one to the other. "Something very bad happened in that room, I'm sure of it. It had all been freshly cleaned, and the cleaning solution must have been very powerful. The smell was overwhelming."

"Did you tell Gareth?" asked Victoria.

"Yes, I told him last night. And you'll never believe what I found there. An earring and I'm pretty sure it belonged to Ashlee. It was wedged down into the crack between the floorboards—not just dropped but placed. I think she was held in that room and had the presence of mind to leave an earring behind so that if the police found it later, they'd know she had been there." Penny was on the brink of telling them she thought Ashlee had been murdered in that room, and then stopped. She could tell Victoria later, but Gwennie might find it too distressing. So instead, she asked Gwennie a question.

"Gwennie, it seems an odd place to have a secure room. What was it used for?"

"Oh, the family used it for anything they wanted to be secure. Confidential papers, Mrs. Gruffydd's jewels, that sort of thing. It's really just a large walk-in closet. It was a bit of leftover space from the renovation when the butler's pantry was put in. I think it was meant to be a wine cellar, but they never installed whatever it is you need to control the temperature and humidity. Mr. Gruffydd, Mr. Rhys, that is, Emyr's father, he enjoyed a glass of wine, but Mrs. Gruffydd wasn't much of a drinker. She had a sherry every now and then, but that was about it. Or sometimes, on a summer afternoon, a gin and tonic in her lovely garden." Gwennie's eyes misted over. "Oh, how I miss her. How I miss those days. Everything seemed so much more beautiful then. We didn't know how good we had it."

The moment passed and with a small sigh she returned to the kitchen.

"Do you think you'll be all right if I go into work this morning?" asked Victoria. "I was thinking you might want to go back to bed."

"I might," said Penny. "But this afternoon I want to drop in on Dilys. I want to make sure she's all right or see if she needs help with anything." She got up from the table and joined Gwennie in the kitchen. "Gwennie, I'm going to check up on Dilys this afternoon and I wondered if you'd mind putting up some sandwiches or something for her. I expect she'll have a lot to do, sorting out the death of her brother."

Gwennie nodded. "Yes, I brought a few things with me, knowing you're not very good at getting in your groceries, although you're better than you used to be, I'll give you that. Very sad it was, what happened to Pawl."

"Yes, it was. Thanks, Gwennie."

Victoria checked her watch. "Look, here's an idea. Why doesn't Gwennie stay here with you for a bit, and I'll go back to the Spa for the morning and make sure everything's all right." She peered out the small window that overlooked the front garden. "It looks like rain. I'll pick you up just after lunch and drive you to see Dilys. We'll go together. After everything that happened yesterday, I don't think you should be on your own, do you?"

Penny shook her head. "No, probably not." She gave her friend a grateful smile.

"Have you spoken to Gareth this morning?"

"Mmm. He rang about an hour ago. Said they'd held everyone in jail overnight and would start interviewing them today." She took another bite of toast. "You know, I'm hungrier than I thought I was. I had breakfast yesterday and that was pretty much all I ate. When I got home last night, I was just too tired to think about food. Just wanted to have a shower and crawl into bed." She brushed the hair from her forehead. "Thanks for stopping over last night. I was so glad to have you here."

"Not the time to be alone," Victoria agreed. "Your spare room's really comfortable. I like the way you've put out the little toiletries and even a new toothbrush. Most people's spare rooms are just a place to keep rubbish they really should get rid of. Stuff that's not really good enough to be in the rest of the house."

She stood up. "Well, I'll leave you to it, then. I'll call Gareth and let him know you're not on your own, and then I'll be back about one thirty and we'll go find Dilys and see how she's doing."

Penny smiled her thanks and picked up her spoon. "Before you go, would you mind asking Gwennie if she'd do me another egg?"

Thirty-three

$\mathcal{A}$ pair of white-suited forensics experts entered the small strong room in Ty Brith Hall, knowing exactly what they were looking for, and in a spray bottle they had what they needed to find it. Luminol. The bottle made a light swooshing sound as they sprayed the carpet and then pulled it back and sprayed the floorboards underneath it. They sprayed the walls. They turned out the light and they waited. A moment later, the carpet, floor, and walls began glowing with an eerie, iridescent blue-green light.

"That stuff gets me every time," one criminalist said to the other, who began photographing and videotaping their findings, including boot prints and spatter patterns. The darling of forensics television shows, luminol reacts with iron in hemoglobin to produce a telltale glow whenever it comes in contact with blood.

The glowing pattern of bloodstains on the walls revealed that a particularly vicious beating had taken place here as an instrument of some kind was raised again and again, casting the victim's blood onto the walls. The carpet had been soaked, allowing the blood to seep through and into the cracks in the floorboards. And in what would no doubt prove invaluable to the investigation, the patterns of two distinct boot treads glowed on the carpet.

"It was bad," one technician remarked to the other. "Brutal. Just brutal."

Thirty-four

*P*enny gazed out the window as fields hemmed in by hedgerows and stone fences flashed by. The snow had disappeared from the lower ground but still clung to the tops of the mountains. A light, persistent drizzle misted the windscreen, and every few minutes Victoria turned on the wipers. Their gentle, rhythmic scraping noise provided an oddly soothing background noise. Trixxi moved restlessly from one side of the car to the other and then sat down and curled up. Penny reached back, between the seats, and gave her a reassuring pat.

"Where was Trixxi while everything was going on?" Victoria asked, breaking the silence.

"They'd put her in the kennels with the other dogs. They got all the dogs out just before the fire really took hold, thank God."

"Other dogs?"

"Yes, there were about half a dozen little dogs in there. Apparently, as a sideline, they were taking people's dogs and selling them on. The dogs were to be taken to the vet today for scanning to see if any were microchipped. The police want to return them to their owners as quickly as possible. Unfortunately, Robbie wasn't with them, though. Thomas and Bronwyn will be disappointed."

"It seems strange that with that big grow op business going on they'd also be stealing dogs."

"Gareth says it's complicated, and they're going to be ages unraveling the finances and everything else that was going on. But he thinks they've got everyone in custody, although Mai and her brother are being held in Birmingham. He says it's going to be a nightmare sorting everyone out. The names are foreign, and everybody's using false identities, anyway."

As they approached the turnoff to Ty Brith Hall, the acrid smell of heavy smoke hung over the landscape. Trixxi resumed her pacing back and forth across the rear seat, whining.

They parked at the front of the house. The stables were cordoned off with police tape, and as they approached, an officer waved.

"That's Chris. Chris Jones. I like him," Penny said to Victoria as they both waved. "They'll still be working on the forensics, I guess." They stopped to look at the building. The grey stone was blackened around the area where the main door used to be.

"I guess because the building is stone the walls are still standing, but just about everything else is gone," Victoria commented.

"The pot smell last night was overpowering," Penny said. "I think we were all a little high, except for the firefighters who had their breathing apparatus."

"What a mess. What a shame. I expect Emyr has been notified and he'll be on his way home. It'll be a lot to sort out. No doubt there'll be a big insurance claim."

"I don't know about that," Penny said as they started off down the path that led to the terraced cottages. "Because there was an illegal activity taking place here, and the wiring had all been jerry-rigged, maybe the insurance won't cover it." She shrugged. "But what do I know?"

"I was surprised that the police blew up the building," Victoria remarked a few minutes later. Penny laughed. "They didn't blow up the building. They had to blow the door off because it was so reinforced they couldn't break it down. And then the building caught fire because of the faulty electrical rigging from the grow op. They're dangerous places, grow ops."

They walked on in silence, Trixxi trotting along beside them and stopping occasionally to sniff an interesting root or branch. They paused outside Pawl's cottage, looked at each other, and then Penny knocked.

A few moments later, Dilys opened the door. She seemed older and stooped, as if under the weight of a heavy burden. Large dark circles under her eyes gave her a hollow, haunted look, and her matted hair was in desperate need of a good brushing. She looked first at Penny and then, with curiosity, at Victoria.

"Oh, it's you," she said to Penny. "You'd better come in. You and your friend."

Penny couldn't bring herself to look at Pawl's chair, so she turned her back to the room as they stood clustered around the doorway. Dilys nodded when Penny introduced Victoria to her.

"We're so very sorry for your loss," Penny said simply.

"Yes, it was terrible the way Pawl went. Dying in a fire must

191

be the worst way to go," Dilys said. "I can't begin to imagine what it must have been like in that inferno—nor do I want to."

"Have you had a chance to think about funeral arrangements?" Victoria asked.

"Nothing to think about," Dilys replied. "Pawl wanted to be cremated and his ashes scattered here, in the Ty Brith gardens, and that's exactly what's going to happen. The police told me there will have to be a postmortem, and then they will release the body. Pawl did not want a fuss and there won't be one."

"We brought you a few groceries," said Penny, holding out a carrier bag filled with sandwiches Gwennie had made, a few bottles of water, some fruit and a couple of yogurts. "Please take it," she added when Dilys hesitated. "Go on."

Dilys took the bag and set it down on her worktable under the window.

"I wondered if we might sit down," Penny said. Dilys nodded. "Dilys, will you be staying on, now that Pawl's gone?"

"I doubt it. The cottage was for Pawl to live in. There's no reason Emyr Gruffydd should allow me to stay on. I expect he'll be back here in the next day or two. He'll have lots to see to, what with the fire and all. And God knows what kind of mess those people left in the house."

"Yes, that's what we were thinking."

Penny gazed at Dilys's table with the old-fashioned weigh scale, mortar and pestle, empty jars with rusting lids, and tattered notebooks with yellowed pages.

"Dilys, I want to ask you something. I've got a feeling you know how Juliette died. I think Pawl knew how she died, and even all these years later it still caused him distress." She leaned forward. "Maybe that knowledge has been a heavy burden for you to carry all these years. I'd like to know how she died, and I hope that if you do know, you'll tell me. Maybe now's the time."

Dilys looked from one to the other and sighed.

"It was the tansy," she said in a low voice. "Tansy tea."

Thirty-five

*P*enny and Victoria exchanged a puzzled glance.

"Tansy tea?" asked Penny. "Is that some kind of herbal tea?"

A pained look crossed Dilys's face. She licked her lips and swallowed.

"It's what we call an abortifacient herb," she said. "It brings on an abortion."

She lowered her eyes.

"Juliette was pregnant, you see. She already had the one boy, he was about six, I think, and she didn't want another child. At least not then. So she came to me, asking for help. I made up the tincture and gave her the tea, and then everything went horribly wrong."

The words hung in the air.

Penny nodded, willing her to continue.

"Very powerful, the tansy is," Dilys said. "You have to know what you're doing. You have to get the dosage right. And God help me, I'll never forgive myself, somehow that time I got it wrong."

Tears welled up and she wiped her eyes with her smooth hands.

"She drank the tea over two or three days and nothing seemed to be happening, so she walked a couple of the dogs down here to see me. It was just before lunch; I remember because I told her Pawl would be along soon for his midday meal and asked her if she wanted to stay and eat with us. She said she did, and then said she wasn't feeling well, so I suggested she lie down in the sitting room while I got the lunch things out. A few moments later, I heard her calling me, and when I got to her, there was blood everywhere.

"At first I wasn't too surprised because you expect that, but when I realized the bleeding wasn't slowing down, I got concerned. She was getting weaker, and just then Pawl came in, hot and tired from his morning's work in the garden, expecting his lunch."

Penny held her breath.

"When he saw the state she was in, he was beside himself. He wanted to run up to the Hall and fetch Mrs. Gruffydd, but what she could have done, I don't know. Anyway"—she made a fluttering gesture—"it was too late. Juliette died."

"And Pawl?" asked Penny.

"He was that upset, as you can imagine." She shook her head. "He knew about the baby, but he didn't know that Juliette had asked me to help her get rid of it. At first, he thought she'd had a natural miscarriage, so he wanted to tell Mrs. Gruffydd. But I had to explain to him what had happened

196

and why we couldn't let anyone know. I would have been arrested and sent to jail."

"So you and Pawl wrapped up the body and hid it?"

"Yes, we did what we had to do. We wrapped her up in a duvet, I think it was, some kind of blanket anyway, and that night we took it to that old building by the river. It was empty. We were just going to leave the body there, but I said, no, let's hide it. So we took off a bit of grillework, it was falling off anyway, and put the body inside."

"And the cat?" asked Victoria. "The body was found with the remains of a cat."

"Oh, that," said Dilys. "I'd forgotten about that. Yes, that was Pawl's doing. He'd found the cat's body that morning behind one of the greenhouses and had planned to bury it that afternoon in the little pet cemetery they had somewhere in the apple orchard. So he decided to put the cat in with Juliette. She loved animals, so he thought it might be comforting to her to have the cat with her, for company, like."

"For company, like," Victoria repeated softly.

"Well, there you have it. My shame and my secret all these years," Dilys said. "In a way, I'm relieved I've finally been able to tell someone. Of course, Pawl hated me afterward, and the atmosphere between us became unbearable, so I had to leave. I didn't see him again for almost forty years, and when I came back, he was so poorly some days he didn't even recognize me."

"But at the time, when Juliette went missing, and everyone was looking for her," Penny asked, "how did you manage to keep the secret and not give yourselves away? Surely everyone who lived or worked at the Hall was questioned."

Dilys shrugged and adjusted the red scarf draped around her

neck. "Well, I wasn't about to say anything, was I, and neither was Pawl. Me and him were family, after all. What good would it have done anyone, least of all him, if I'd been banged up in prison? Would that bring her back?"

"It's a lot to take in and I don't know what to say," said Penny.

Dilys sat back in her chair and sighed. "I suppose you'll be telling the authorities?"

Penny said nothing. Victoria was about to say something, but Penny shot her a warning glance accompanied by a slight shake of her head.

"It doesn't matter to me if you do," said Dilys. "I'll just deny everything, and they won't be able to prove anything after all this time."

Penny remained silent.

"Well?" said Victoria as they fastened their seat belts.

"I don't know what to make of it. What do you think?"

"It's a problem, that's for sure. Dilys is old, all this happened a long time ago, she's just lost her brother in a terrible way. Would punishing her now change anything? And maybe she's been punishing herself all these years. She doesn't seem like a callous person."

"No, but she didn't seem particularly remorseful, either, did she? And then there's the question of justice for Juliette. All those years her body lay there in the ductwork of a decrepit old building. She was taken away from her child, who must have spent his whole life wondering what happened to her. And Pawl lost his child."

A determined look crossed Penny's face. "No. Why should

we keep her secret? Why should we have to live with it? That would make us just as guilty as she is. I'll tell Gareth tonight. No more secrets."

Victoria slowed down as her car reached the end of the winding road that led down from Ty Brith, checked the road ahead for oncoming traffic, and then turned onto the motorway that would take them home to Llanelen. "The thing is, though, I expect by the time Gareth gets up there to talk to her, she'll be gone again. She disappeared once before for a very long time, and she can do it again."

Penny gave her a sharp look and pulled her mobile out of her handbag. "Do we know where she was all those years?" asked Victoria as Penny pressed the call button on her mobile. "Wherever she was, I expect she'll be going back there anyway. She likely won't be able to stay on in the cottage now that Pawl's gone. Emyr gave permission for him to live there, not his sister."

Victoria listened as Penny described to Gareth the conversation they had just had with Dilys. He asked a few questions and then Penny ended the call.

"Well?"

"He's sending Chris Jones over to talk to her. Chris is at the Hall, so he'll be there in a few minutes and Bethan's on her way to join him. But I expect you're right. Dilys is probably packing now, and she'll have moved on by the end of the day."

Glad of the chance to stretch his legs, Jones set off along the path that wound its way to the terraced workers' cottages. In the last hour an ominous mist had settled over the tops of the Snowdonia Mountains, giving them a secretive look, and a heavy, patchy fog had come swirling down the valley, blanketing everything it touched in a shroud of Celtic mystery. As he passed the small copse of beech trees that separated the formal gardens near the Hall from the pastures and wildflower meadows beyond the workers' cottages, he could barely make out the interwoven pattern of the black branches silhouetted against the pewter sky as the fading afternoon light seeped between the branches. And then a flash of scarlet, strident and bold against the dour, neutral tones of black and grey, caught his attention. Afterward, he would say he could barely see it, and at first he thought it was the fluttering of a piece of cloth, caught on a branch. But as he came closer, peering through the fog, he saw it was a scarf draped over the branch and, hanging from it, the body of a grey-haired woman, turning slowly, her shabby boots barely skimming the ground. Every turn added another twist to the knotted red scarf that suspended her, tightening the tourniquet around her swollen, purple neck.

"How's Chris doing?" Penny asked as she held out a glass of beer to Davies. "He's holding up," Davies replied, before taking a grateful sip and then licking his top lip. "What he saw with that woman is not something anyone should have to see, but it was a great thing that he got there in time to save her. A few minutes later and who knows?"

"And do you think it was an attempted suicide?"

"Well, I'm not sure at this point," he said cautiously. "We haven't been able to interview her yet as she's still unconscious, but the doctors are cautiously optimistic she'll recover."

"I thought so," said Penny. "There's more to it. She didn't seem the least bit suicidal when we left her."

She stood in front of him with her arms crossed over her chest. "You look tired. How about something warm and comforting for supper?"

He reached up for her hand. "I'd love that. Exactly what I need."

"Good. Gwennie's left some of her leek and potato soup and I'll do some grilled cheese. And then you can tell me about Dilys."

While Penny prepared their simple meal, Gareth switched on the television to watch the news. The hanging at the Hall was not mentioned.

Gareth brought in a plate of slices of crusty bread dripping with melted cheese as Penny ladled the soup into bowls. She returned the pot to the kitchen and came back to the table holding a lit candle, which she placed in the centre of the table.

"A little touch of atmosphere." She smiled.

As they tucked into their meal, Penny grimaced.

"What is it?"

"I just had an image of what poor Dilys must have looked like before Chris got her down." She shuddered. "I don't think there can be a more grisly way to take your own life than hanging." She gave Gareth a meaningful look. "Especially if you didn't have to."

"Meaning what?"

"Well, Dilys had a wealth of knowledge of herbs and plants. She would know which ones are poisonous. If she had really wanted to top herself, I don't think she'd choose hanging. No, she'd go for a toxic dose of something powerful that would be fast. I doubt very much she was trying to kill herself. She was sad about Pawl but not desperately so. Not enough to kill herself, if you know what I mean."

Gareth nodded. "I do know what you mean."

Penny looked at him with narrowed eyes.

"Did she leave a suicide note?"

"A note was found, yes."

"That's an odd answer. What do you mean?"

"A note was found, or rather, left for us to find, but I don't think she wrote it."

"Because?"

"Because when I asked her last night for her brother's name, she spelled it for me. P-A-W-L. The Welsh way. In the note it was spelled the English way. P-A-U-L."

Penny sprang from the table and sprinted up the stairs. A few moments later she returned and handed Davies a piece of paper.

"Here. You can compare the handwriting on the suicide note to this. I saw her write this with my own eyes. This is her handwriting."

Davies read from the scrap of paper in his hand. *Valerian. For sleep. Mix one teaspoon in glass of warm water and take at bedtime. Do not exceed dosage in one night.*

Thirty-six

"So is everybody under arrest, then?" Victoria asked the next morning.

"Mai and her brother will stay in custody in Birmingham," Penny said. "Apparently he ran the operation and was the brains behind it and she was the banker. She managed the money."

"And the husband and son?"

"They're still being questioned, but the police aren't sure yet about the extent of their involvement and how much they knew, although they had to have known something. They were living in the same house and they aren't stupid." The door to the small staff room opened and Rhian, the receptionist, poked her head in.

"Sorry to bother you, Penny," she said, "but the first client of the day is here for her manicure and Eirlys hasn't arrived. I'm a bit worried, to be honest. It's not like her not to let me know she was going to be late. You know how reliable and steady she is.

She . . . oh." Rhian took a step back and glanced down the hall. "Never mind. It's all right. Here she is now." She gave Penny a relieved grin before closing the door.

Penny frowned. "I'd better see to this."

Victoria stood up. "I have to pay the suppliers today, so I'd best get on."

"Eirlys? Is everything all right?" Penny stood behind her young manicurist in the supply room and watched as she poured some herbal salts into a small bowl. Keeping her back to Penny, Eirlys walked the few steps to the sink and ran the hot water. She ran a finger under the stream and then filled the bowl. As fragrant steam rose around them, she turned to Penny and placed a shaking hand under the bowl to steady it. But the bowl was hot and she pulled her hand away quickly, with a little gasp. Penny leaped forward. "Here, give that to me."

She took the bowl and set it on the counter. "Eirlys, look at me."

Eirlys raised her red, puffy eyes but could not meet Penny's gaze.

"Look, we can't keep the customer waiting, so we've got about two minutes. Okay?" She covered the bowl with a clean towel.

"Right. Tell me what's the matter. I want to help."

"It's Trefor," Eirlys said in a low voice. "My brother. He's in a lot of bother."

"What kind of bother?"

"He got mixed up with that awful Tyler Tran and he's done something bad." Her eyes swam with tears. "I think I know where he was getting that money to buy the video games and things."

"Tell me, Eirlys," Penny said softly. "What's he done?"

Eirlys lowered her gage and then whispered, "He stole those dogs."

"Do you know this for sure?"

Eirlys shook her head. "Not for absolutely sure, but I think that's what it is."

"Right. We need to talk to him. Where is he now?"

"At school."

"Does he come home for lunch?"

Eirlys nodded.

"Okay. Here's what we'll do. I don't think you're in any shape to deliver a professional client experience right now. I want you to go home. Is your mum at home this morning?"

Eirlys nodded.

"Good, because it wouldn't be right if I talked to Trefor without her permission. You go home and tell her I've asked if I can have a word with him at lunchtime. Send me a text and let me know what she says. When you feel better, when you've got yourself composed, you come back and we'll go together to see Trefor at lunchtime."

Eirlys nodded gratefully.

"Sound like a plan, then?" Eirlys gave a watery smile and started to wipe her eyes with her fingers.

Penny cleared her throat.

"Sorry, Penny, I know you don't like that. I wasn't thinking." Eirlys accepted the tissues Penny handed her.

"Right, you get off home. I'll explain to your client and do her manicure."

Just after noon the kitchen door opened, and Eirlys's younger brother, Trefor, pushed his way into the warm kitchen. He glanced at Penny and gave his mother a quizzical look. She gave him a warm smile.

"Hello, love. Penny's here and wants a word with you."

She got up from the table and busied herself warming up a tin of tomato soup and making a ham sandwich. The soft domestic sounds of the refrigerator door opening, a drawer closing, and a loaf of bread being unwrapped made everything seem ordinary and calm.

"What about?" Trefor asked cautiously.

"Trefor, a dog belonging to two very dear friends of mine has gone missing," Penny began. "They both loved him very much. A little cairn terrier called Robbie. They asked me to help them get their dog back, and I think you might know something." She reached into her handbag and from between the pages of her diary pulled out the photograph of Robbie the rector had given her, taken at Christmas. It was almost a close-up of his face, and his collar, with a distinctive dog tag, was clearly visible. "Trefor, look at this photo. Have you seen this dog? Do you know what happened to him?"

A look of fear mixed with defiance flashed across his face, but he said nothing. Penny glanced at his mother, who had turned around and, with the small knife she was holding, gestured at her son.

"Trefor," she said, "we're waiting."

The boy shut his eyes and tears leaked from his closed lids.

"Tell me," said Penny as she signaled to his mother for a tissue. "Tell me what happened."

"I had to do it, Mum!" he cried. "He said he'd do awful things to Eirlys if I didn't. And I believed him. He's mean and he would have done them, I know he would."

He blew his nose. "He enjoyed taking those dogs. He thought it was fun. He said the best bit was watching the look on people's faces when they realized their dog was gone. It made him laugh."

He jumped up from the table and ran to his room. A few moments later, he returned with a small biscuit tin. "Here," he said, holding it out to Penny. She lifted the lid and saw five dog tags, one of which, in the shape of a bone with a little red Welsh dragon on it, she recognized. She turned it over and ran her finger lightly over the inscription. ROBBIE.

"Where is Robbie, Trefor? What happened to him? What did you do with him?"

Trefor's mother placed the sandwich in front of her son and sat down.

"We sold him to a couple," Trefor said in a low voice. "I don't know where he is now." He pushed the sandwich away and buried his face in his fingers. "If I could bring him back, I would." He snuffled into his hands. "I'm so sorry."

"Yes, well, you need to try to remember everything you can about this couple," said Penny. "How did you find them? Where did you meet them? Did you hand over the dog to them?"

"Tyler put an ad on one of those online sites," said Trefor, "and the couple answered it and said they wanted a dog. So we met them at the cricket ground and handed over the dog." He shrugged. "I don't know anything about them. They were old, that's all."

"How old are you, Trefor?"

"Fourteen."

Penny looked at the boy's mother and raised an eyebrow. To a fourteen-year-old, anyone over thirty would probably be classified as old.

"Right, then. Did you talk to these people? Were they English or Welsh, do you think?"

Trefor brightened. "The man was Welsh. The woman, I'm not sure about her." He thought for a moment and then raised a finger. "Yes, there was something else. I remember now. The woman, she said to the man, you don't think the B and B guests will mind another dog, do you?"

"So you think they were staying at a B and B, do you?"

"No, from the way she said it, but I can't remember her exact words, it sounded like they owned the B and B."

"Did you watch them leave with the dog?"

"Not really."

"So you don't know which direction they drove off in?"

He pinched his lips together and slowly shook his head.

Penny lifted her hands in a vague gesture as if to signal there was nothing more to be said. And then Trefor spoke again.

"I didn't watch them drive off, but I know where they were going."

Penny's head snapped back.

"You do?"

"Yes, the woman said they'd better get back to Betws before the shops closed because she needed 'milk for the morning.' That's what she said. 'Milk for the morning.'"

Penny stood up. "Well, you've been very helpful, Trefor. Thank you."

Trefor gave his mother an anxious glance and then turned a fearful gaze to Penny.

"Will you be telling your policeman friend about this, then?"

Penny nodded. "Yes, Trefor, I will. We're going to need his help to get the dog back. But I'll also tell him how helpful you were. And he may have some questions of his own for you."

"Will I be going to prison, do you think?"

Penny smiled. "No, I don't think you will. As long as you don't go looking for trouble and steer clear of bad lads who will bring you down with them."

"She's right about that," his mother said. "Now eat your sandwich and get ready to go back to school while I see Penny out."

In Llandudno, DCI Davies replaced the telephone receiver and turned to his sergeant, Bethan Morgan.

"Sergeant, I need you to ring round the B and Bs in Betws and surrounding area. Tell them you're looking for accommodation but you're allergic to dogs and there can't be any dogs on the premises. And then make a list of all the ones that have dogs."

"So I'm looking for a B and B that doesn't take dogs."

"No, you're looking for all the B and Bs that do have dogs." He related the information Penny had just learned from Trefor.

"It seems the rector's dog, Robbie, may have been sold on to a couple operating a B and B in the Betws area. If you can give me a list of the ones with dogs, we'll try to narrow it down. It's very likely the couple who bought him didn't know he'd been stolen, and they'll be shocked and disappointed when they find out. But our priority is returning him to the Evanses as soon as we can. And the other dogs, to their rightful owners, too.

"You'll have to follow up with young Trefor and see what you can find out about the other dogs. But for now, let's concentrate on getting Robbie back.

"So ring round the B and Bs and once you've done that, Penny and I'll be taking a nice drive in the country."

Thirty-seven

*B*y late afternoon Davies had a list of five bed-and-breakfast establishments in the Betws Y Coed area that kept dogs, and with Penny in the passenger seat of an unmarked police car and Trixxi in the back, they set off to call on them.

The day had started out grey and gloomy with light snow showers bringing some hill fog, but the weather can change quickly in North Wales. Now, with a brisk wind blowing in from the sea and over the mountains and the sky turning the palest of blues, the air was crisp and clear.

"We got the results back on the marijuana seized at the Hall," Davies said as they passed the turnoff to Ty Brith Hall, "and this might interest you. The plants were B.C. Bud. It's a particularly potent strain. Almost twenty percent TCP."

"TCP, that's the—"

"Part of the plant that gets you high. So we've been in touch with the RCMP's drug squad. Seems your lot is now exporting pot seeds. They're into marijuana in a big way, actually. There's a whole town in British Columbia whose economy is based on growing marijuana. They call it cannabiz."

"They're not my lot! I've lived here so long I barely think of myself as Canadian. I don't know what I am, anymore." She gazed out the window as grey rocks and woodland flew by.

"And Ashlee," she said a few minutes later. "Any news on that investigation?"

"Well, we have the DNA results on the fetus. The father isn't someone we have on record. But the blood in the strong room was hers. You were right about that. Something very bad did happen there."

He threw her a quick glance and then reached over for her hand. "I'm just so glad that two very bad things didn't happen there."

They drove on in silence for a few more kilometres, then Davies slowed down as he turned off the Betws Road, and they crossed the Waterloo Bridge and entered the town.

With its perfectly scenic location at the confluence of three rivers and three forested valleys at the edge of Snowdonia National Park, the town bustled from early spring to late fall with cyclists, climbers, hikers, tourists, and sightseers. In winter, the town was eerily quiet and locals were left to themselves. Passing a couple of grey stone hotels, they drove along beside the river until they reached the sign that marked the entrance to a Victorian guesthouse.

"Here we go," said Penny, peering up at the grey gables through the slightly misted car window. The sound of the ringing doorbell triggered loud, deep barking from somewhere in the depths of the house. A few moments later, they heard the sound of approaching footsteps, accompanied by a man's voice saying, "All right then, Hugo, settle down," and then the door swung open, revealing a stocky, middle-aged man dressed in an old-fashioned pair of grey flannel trousers, a white shirt, green cardigan, and a striped tie. A handsome dog, its front paw wrapped in bright pink surgical bandage, which contrasted beautifully with its curly, black fur, waited beside him, panting and sizing up the visitors with expressive eyes.

"Good afternoon. May I help you?"

"I hope so," said Davies. "We've not come about accommodation, but we've come about a dog."

The man's eyes narrowed and he tilted his head to one side as he echoed, "A dog? What about a dog?"

Davies explained the situation of stolen dogs and waited for the man to respond.

"I'm sorry I can't help you. We do have a dog, but as you can see, he doesn't fit your description."

"Right," said Davies. "Do you know anyone who has recently acquired a cairn terrier?"

The man pursed his lips and shook his head.

"No, sorry, can't say as I do."

They thanked him and returned to the car. After four more tries, they had reached the end of the guesthouses on the list Bethan had given them, with no luck.

"How would you feel about having dinner before we head back to Llanelen?" Davies asked. "I know it's early, but the Royal Oak does a nice roast chicken. Might really hit the spot for dinner tonight."

"I am getting hungry," Penny agreed, "but I'm so disappointed we weren't able to find Robbie. I really thought we might."

"I know, love, but we'll keep looking."

They strolled along to the hotel and entered its comfortable reception area. A sign in front of the dining room giving the hours of dinner service let them know they had arrived about half an hour too early.

"Should we have a drink at the bar while we wait?" Davies asked.

"I think I'd rather have a glass of wine with dinner," replied Penny. "How about a walk down by the river and perhaps along the boardwalk before it gets dark?"

"Sounds good." Davies smiled as he held the door open for her. They crossed the street and made their way across the bridge that spanned the Llugwy River with its jagged rocks and churning water until they came to the raised boardwalk that meandered under the trees and sometimes even around them.

The late afternoon sunlight slanted through the trees, creating cascades of muted light and shadow.

"The days are getting noticeably longer now," Davies observed, glancing upward at the boughs of evergreens shifting slightly in the wind.

"Hmm," said Penny as she prepared to step to one side to let a woman walking two dogs pass.

Dressed in a burgundy coat, the woman, who appeared to be in her sixties, gave Penny a quick smile and then stopped in front of her, speaking to one of her dogs that had stopped to sniff a sandwich wrapper. "Come on, Pip, leave it. We don't want to be late."

"Hello," said Penny, before bending down to give the dogs a pat. She straightened up and then spoke to the woman. "I wonder if you can help us. We're looking for someone walking a dog that looks like this and wondered if you might have seen them out and about." Penny showed her the photo of Robbie. "But I think from your accent you might be an American, so perhaps you . . ."

"No, I live here," the woman said. "Well, in Conwy. My husband's Welsh. We've just been having an afternoon out." She looked at the photo and then gestured back the way she had come.

"A woman passed me about five minutes ago with a dog that looked a lot like that. A cairn terrier, is it? He was wearing a little red coat." She smiled. "Or she. I just think of dogs as male because mine are." A worried frown crossed her kind face. "Not lost, I hope?"

Davies and Penny exchanged quick glances. "Maybe if we hurry, we can catch her up," Penny said.

"You may not have to chase after her," the woman said, "because the boardwalk ends and she'll have to come back this way." She shrugged. "It's a pleasant walk, but it doesn't really go anywhere. Well, there is a footpath that continues after the boardwalk ends, but it goes through a sheep pasture and is bound to be terribly muddy at this time of year, so I doubt she'd go there."

"So you think if we . . ."

"Well, you could walk on a bit and you'll meet her coming back that much sooner, I suppose."

"Thank you," said Penny. "You've been really helpful." She bent down again to give the other dog a pat. "And who's this?"

"That's Jocan. He's part corgi, we think."

They exchanged good-byes and the woman turned to go, with an encouraging, "Come on, boys, time to go home." She met her husband in the car park, and as they were putting the dogs in the car the woman remarked, "I met a Canadian woman looking for a lost dog. You can always tell a Canadian by the way they say 'about.'"

As she settled herself in the passenger side, her husband asked, "Well, I hope they find the dog. Now, then, Sylvia, what should we do about dinner?"

As the American woman had predicted, a few minutes later a woman leading a small dog came into view on the boardwalk. Penny clutched Davies' arm and then, out of the corner of her eye, she caught a glimpse of movement, which she realized was him reaching into his breast pocket. As she approached Penny and Davies, the woman walked a little faster. She kept her head down and did not look at them, and then just as she was about to pass them, with a quick, unexpected movement, Davies blocked her path.

"Excuse me, ma'am," he said, holding up his warrant card. "I'd like to talk to you about that dog. We have reason to believe it was stolen."

A fake smile slid across the woman's lips.

"Nonsense. Now let me pass."

"Can you tell me where you got the dog, please?"

"No, I don't have to speak to you."

"Very well, then. If you'd rather, we can continue this conversation at the police station in Llanelen. Or you can answer my questions now."

She gave him a defiant look, but a few moments later her

shoulders sank and she glanced down at the dog, who was wagging his tail with excitement while Penny stroked him.

"I didn't steal the dog. We paid good money for him."

"Did you get him from a couple of lads in Llanelen?"

The woman said nothing, so Davies repeated the question and added, "And if you did, would you describe them, please."

Accepting that her best bet now was cooperation, the woman sighed.

"Well, there were two of them. Our other dog is getting on a bit, and we thought we'd like to get a younger dog but not a puppy. And then we saw an advert for a terrier on one of those Web sites, you know, where people buy and sell stuff. So we contacted the seller."

"How did you contact him?" Davies interrupted.

"By phone. There was a phone number in the ad, so we rang the number and arranged to meet at the cricket ground. He said to bring a hundred pounds in cash, and if we liked the dog we could take him home with us—and that's what happened."

"Tell me about the boys."

"They were young teenagers, one a bit older than the other. Chinese, he looked like. Or Korean, maybe? I don't know. I hate to sound racist, but those people all look alike to me. I can't tell the difference."

"I don't suppose they gave you a receipt or anything in writing to prove you paid for the dog?" The woman shook her head. "No," said Davies. "I thought not." Penny, who had been stroking the dog, gave him one last pat and stood up.

"Ma'am, we're going to take this dog to a vet," Davies said. "The dog we're looking for is microchipped. If this is the dog we think it is, you'll not be seeing him again. If it isn't the dog, we will continue our investigation. Now, may I have your address, please?"

As she gave her address, Davies' expression tightened. "We spoke to your husband earlier and inquired about this dog. Lying to the police is a serious offence, and he can expect a visit from a police officer to discuss that. But in the meantime, as I said, we're going to get this dog checked."

Penny glared at her. "How could you take a beautiful dog off a couple of lads and not know the dog had been stolen?" she demanded. "Where did they tell you they got it? What kind of story did they tell you?"

"I don't think I'm going to say anything unless I have a solicitor present," the woman said, as tears filled her eyes. "Can I say good-bye to him? We haven't had him very long, but I've become so fond of him. I bought that coat for him. He's a lovely wee boy."

"His real owners, who are missing him terribly, also think he's a lovely wee boy," Penny couldn't resist saying.

Davies held his hand out to the woman, and with obvious reluctance she placed the dog's lead in it. As he handed the lead to Penny, he gave the woman a brief, tight nod. "You may go now. But do tell your husband to expect a visit. Lying to a police officer wastes time and in serious cases can put people in harm's way. We take a dim view of it. And the officer will want to know where you got the black dog, so if you've got papers or a bill of sale for him, best dig it out."

When the woman had taken a few steps, he placed a call. He listened for a moment, then rang off. "They're making arrangements for Jones the vet to meet us at the surgery in an hour."

He put a sheltering arm around Penny, and as the light began to fade and the first faint splashes of pink began to streak across the evening sky, they walked slowly to his car. He settled Penny and her precious bundle into the backseat beside Trixxi, and with one last glance to make sure they were all sorted, he climbed into the driver's seat.

The pale pink darkened into a deep rosy glow, and dark shadows began to engulf the scenery around them.

Jones the vet ran a handheld scanner over the dog's back. "This dog has been microchipped, so that's a good thing," he said, as a number came up. He entered the number into a database as Penny held her hand over her mouth. Jones gave the dog a little pat and smiled.

"Just as I thought," he said. "This charming character is registered to the rector, but I suspect it's really Bronwyn who owns him," he confirmed. "This is Robbie." A little sob caught in Penny's throat as Davies put his arm around her.

Penny cradled Robbie in her arms, rubbing her chin on his head, as Davies knocked on the rectory door. They grinned at each other, and their smiles widened as footsteps approached. A moment later, Bronwyn opened the door, and seeing the precious bundle in Penny's arms, she gave a little yelp and reached for him. She buried her face in his fur, and then, her eyes glistening, she gestured to the two to come in. She set Robbie down on the hall carpet and called for her husband.

"Thomas, come here at once! It's our Robbie. Penny's brought him home!"

As Robbie trotted off down the hall toward the kitchen, the rector rushed down the hall from his study, buttoning his cardigan.

Thirty-eight

"Run that by me again, Penny." The two business partners had worked late, poring over the end-of-the-month accounts, and decided to stop in the local pub, the Leek and Lily, on the way home.

"I can't see how the grow op and the dog thefts are connected to Ashlee's murder, can you? But everything happened at the Hall, within the same family, so there has to be something."

Victoria was about to speak and then tilted her head. "What's that?"

"Sounds like someone shouting."

As they rounded the corner into the town square, two men came spilling out of the pub. The larger man drew his fist back and smashed the smaller one square in the face. As his victim's hands covered his gushing nose, the larger man shouted at him, "I catch you sniffing around my wife again, you bleedin' sod, I'll swing for you."

Other men from the pub had now caught up with them and, pinning the larger man by his arms, pulled him back. "Come on, now, Glyn," one of them said, "let's be having you. Any more of this and the cops'll be here. He's not worth it. Leave him be."

With one last glare over his shoulder, and muttering vague threats as he went, Glyn and his supporters disappeared back into the pub, leaving their victim standing unsteadily looking about. He leaned against the building and closed his eyes.

Penny reached into her handbag and pulled out a packet of tissues as the two women crossed the street.

"Here." Penny held out a few tissues. "They're clean," she added as he opened his eyes. "Oh, right. Cheers." He wiped his bloodied nose. "Hello, ladies. Ta very much." He brightened. "Two lovely ladies to the rescue." His eyes swept up and down Victoria, lingering for a moment, and then moved on to Penny.

"So what was that all about, then?" she asked.

"Oh, he thinks I've been eyeing up his missus. As if! Spent all her time in that tanning place while it was open. Tanning! Tannery, more like. Got an orange hide on her like a cheap handbag."

Victoria held up a finger and seemed about to say something and then caught herself.

The man folded the tissues over, dabbed at his nose, and then examined the results. Satisfied that the bleeding was slowing down he looked around for a rubbish bin. Seeing none within arm's length, he seemed about to toss the bloody tissues on the pavement so Penny reached in her pocket and held out a small bag. "Just put them in here and I'll get rid of them for you."

"Oh, right." He dropped them in the bag and then gazed

longingly at the pub. "Well, I guess there's no point in going back in there. Might as well head home. My missus'll be wondering what's happened to me." He gave a sheepish smile and strolled off.

"Creeps me out when men do that," Penny remarked as they watched him go. "That eyeing you up and down."

"I know him," Victoria said. "Or at least I know who he is I thought for a moment he was about to recognize me. I've seen him before and you'll never guess where."

"Tell me, then."

"In the kitchen of Ty Brith Hall. He was with the family when I was up there pretending to be a cleaner."

"Really?"

"Yes, really. Oh, what was his name? Oh, damn. Starts with *B*."

"Do we still want to go to the pub?" Penny asked. "Why don't we pick up a bottle of wine and something to eat and go back to yours? I'm sure his name will come to you."

"Good idea."

Their shopping done, they walked past the now shuttered Handz and Tanz back toward the Spa to Victoria's comfortable flat on the top floor.

"I wonder where everybody who used to work there went," Victoria remarked, with a little gesture at the closed nail and tanning salon.

"Gareth says the whole business is a tangled mess of extortion, people-smuggling, money laundering, and prostitution, not to mention the grow op. Where there are drugs, there are guns, he said. They're still working with the police in Birmingham to sort it all out. They've got some of the gang in custody, but there are more back in Birmingham and some have probably left the country.

"Oh, and remember that boy who was in the stables? Trung, I think he said his name was. He's been taken into care, and Gareth said that's actually the second time they've picked him up. They caught him once before working at another grow op, but he ran away. They think he was smuggled into the country just so he could work in the grow op, looking after the plants. Sad, that."

As they passed a rubbish bin, Penny reached in her pocket, pulled out the bag containing the bloody tissues, and dropped it in.

They walked on, and just as the Spa came into sight, Penny stopped, thought for a moment, then turned around and walked back to the rubbish bin and picked up the bag.

Thirty-nine

"While you're heating up dinner I'm going to phone Gareth," she called to Victoria in the kitchen. A few minutes later, she joined Victoria, who handed her a couple of plates.

"Better make it one more," Penny said. "He refused to talk to me on the phone. Said he couldn't. Told him we were about to have dinner and he invited himself over." She gestured at the meal Victoria was preparing. "I thought you wouldn't mind. Can we stretch it to three, do you think?"

"'Course we can. Unlike you, I always have food in." She opened the fridge door and started handing out things. "Here's some cheese, there are bread rolls in the freezer, and there'll be tons of pasta. Oh, look, here's a red pepper. I'll chop that up and toss it in the salad."

"He said he'd pick up a bottle of wine."

"Well, that's good, then. We're all set."

"Hello, love. How are you? All right?"

"Mmm, fine. You?"

"Good." He handed his coat and a bottle of wine to Penny with a gentle smile and the two of them walked into the sitting room. "Dinner'll be ready in just a few minutes," said Victoria, handing Penny some cutlery. "Just put those out, please, and, Gareth, perhaps you'd be good enough to pour us some wine."

A few minutes later, they were seated, and Victoria passed the large bowl of pasta to Davies. "This looks delicious," Davies said as he helped himself. "I'm hungry."

Victoria reached for the basket of warm bread rolls and passed them to Penny. As Penny took the basket from her, the two exchanged subtle glances and Victoria gave a tiny nod.

"Now then, Gareth," Penny began. He looked up from his plate. "Victoria and I had an interesting encounter just outside the pub today." He raised an eyebrow. "Yes, we met a fellow who had been set upon by a jealous husband. And it turns out that Victoria met this fellow a few weeks ago—in the kitchen of Ty Brith Hall, of all places."

"That's right," chimed in Victoria. "He was well in with the family, it looked to me. Very comfortable. Sitting at the table, drinking tea."

"What were you doing up there?" Gareth asked.

Victoria and Penny exchanged nervous glances.

"Nothing much, really," Victoria said. "We just wanted to see if we could find out a bit more about their business plans. When they first opened their nail bar we were a little nervous about the competition, you see. But it turned out their clients weren't our clients, so it was no threat to our business."

Davies put down his fork. "So you were up there and met the family? Of course, you weren't to know, but that could have been dangerous for you, very dangerous if you'd seen or heard something you shouldn't have. There was a lot of illegal activity going on, and these gangs mean business. They are not the forgiving type."

"Do you think that's what happened to Ashlee? That she saw or heard something?"

"We don't know how much the kids knew, but they were old enough to know something was going on. There would have been lots of traffic with collectors showing up, and everybody would have had to be kept away from the grow op."

"Collectors?"

"In the drug trade, collectors pick up product from the growers and move it to the distributors. It's a very sophisticated business now." He took a sip of wine. "You know, ten years ago about ninety percent of the illegal drugs in Britain were imported. Now, it's just about all homegrown or homemade. It's a multibillion-pound business. There's a lot of money at stake and this operation was huge. The plants alone were worth millions. It's going to be difficult sorting it all out." He let out a weary sigh. "Oh, how we long for the good old days of the Kray Brothers. At least back then, our criminals were British, we all spoke the same language, and everybody knew the rules. Now, we're up against Eastern European and Asian gangs, so it's not easy for us poor old plods."

Penny leaned forward. "Go on."

"Well, it's almost impossible for us to infiltrate these gangs. We're working with the RCMP on this case, because the plants come from Canada. There could be a connection to the big grow ops in British Columbia."

"Hmm. Interesting. But I've been thinking about that blond good-looking man in the kitchen, who's close to the family. The same one Penny and I saw fighting outside the pub. Remembered his name. Bruno he's called. Could he have had anything to do with Ashlee's death, do you think?"

Davies thought for a moment.

"We've looked into him, of course."

"And?"

"And he's an old friend of Derek's. We found him useful."

"Useful? Useful how?"

"He's a police informant. Or was. He was working for us. That's how we knew so much about the grow op.

"But . . ." Davies held up his hands in a good-natured way. "That's all I'm going to say. That's all I can say."

Davies set down his coffee cup and stood up. "That was lovely, Victoria, thanks so much, but now I must be off. Meeting in Birmingham in the morning." He looked at Penny. "Am I driving you home?"

"No, I think I'll stay here for a bit and help Victoria tidy up."

"I'm fine, Penny, honestly, you go home now."

"I'd like to stay for a bit."

"Well, all right, but what about Trixxi?"

"Gwennie's been over to walk her, she'll have fed her. She'll be fine. I'll just see Gareth out and then I'll help with the clearing up." Victoria picked up a tray and began piling the coffee cups on it.

A few moments later, Penny joined her in the kitchen.

"Leave the dishes for a few minutes and come into the sitting room." Victoria turned off the tap, and wiping her hands on a small white towel that looked suspiciously like the ones in the Spa, she followed Penny into the sitting room. When they were seated, Penny leaned forward.

"I need to talk this through with you. I think Gareth's wrong about Bruno. Here's my theory. When Ashlee came to me for the snakeskin manicure she told me how unhappy she was here in Llanelen, and I said something like, well, maybe you'll meet a nice lad. And she said, oh, I'm not interested in boys. And I thought she meant she wasn't interested in boys—"

"That she was interested in girls," Victoria finished for her.

"Exactly. But now, I think she meant she wasn't interested in boys, she—"

"Was interested in men." Victoria finished for her again. "I see where you're going with this."

"Yes. There was something about the way she said it. A certain smugness. I think she was very pleased with herself because she had the attentions of a man who must be, what, in his early thirties?"

"And apparently she wasn't terribly good-looking, so it must have all been very exciting for her."

"He probably told her all kinds of lies, everything she wanted to hear, but for him it was all just a bit of fun. You know what men like that are like. But when she told him she'd fallen pregnant, it all went wrong. Maybe she threatened to tell his wife. Maybe he laughed at her and mocked her."

"I think he killed her in that little room."

"I think you came pretty close to getting killed in that little room yourself."

"I don't think her death had anything to do with the grow op. I think she was killed because of the pregnancy."

"And what about Dilys?"

"I think she saw something. Or knew something." She snapped her fingers. "That's it! She knew that Bruno was the father of Ashlee's baby because he asked her for something to get rid of it. Like that tansy tea."

"But why would he do that?" Before Penny could reply, she answered her own question. "Of course. Because Ashlee liked being pregnant. It gave her a hold over him and she would never have consented to an abortion."

"Exactly!"

They looked at each other, the excitement between them growing. "But how would he have known that Dilys knew about that sort of thing? That she had access to those types of herbs?" They thought about that.

"Well, she lived in the cottage just down from the main house. He might have bumped into her one day when she was coming back through the fields after a foraging mission with her basket full of plants and got talking to her. I'll bet he can be very charming on a good day and when he wants to be."

Victoria nodded.

"And persuasive."

"So what do you think we should do next?"

"Well, for starters, we have to be very careful. If we're right, and I think we are, we know he's dangerous. We can't confront him, that's for sure. So we have to find some proof to give to Gareth so he'll believe us."

"And we have the tissues with the blood so they can run a DNA test."

"True."

Penny stood up. "Do you like gambling?"

"Not particularly. Why?"

"Because one of us has to visit the bookies in the morning."

"You go. I'll take care of the business."

Forty

The overhead bell tinkled as Penny opened the door to the bookmaker's. A few customers watching the television screens took no notice of her as she walked to the counter at the rear of the shop.

"Hello," she said to the clerk. "I wondered if I could speak to, well, I'm afraid I don't know his name. You see, I saw a little dustup outside the pub yesterday between—"

"Oh, that." He turned toward the back room. "Glyn! Lady here wants a word."

A few moments later, the man who had been fighting in the street emerged, carrying a mug of tea, which he set down on the counter before making eye contact with Penny.

"Yes?"

"Hello. My name's Penny Brannigan and I wondered if could ask you a couple of questions about that incident outside the pub yesterday." She glanced at the other man and seemed unsure whether to continue. "You were having a disagreement with, I think his first name is Bruno, but I don't know his last name, sorry."

"Bishop, would you believe. That's his last name. What about him?"

"I overheard what you said about him being interested in your wife and I just wondered—"

"He's not particularly interested in her," Glyn replied, emphasizing the word "her." "He's interested in anything in a skirt." He looked at the man beside him. "Do women still wear skirts?" And then back to Penny. "Well, you know what I mean. Some towns have a drunk, some villages have an idiot, apparently we have our womanizer. I told him to clear off and I think he heard me, loud and clear."

His colleague nodded. "You're right about that, Glyn, he got the message, loud and clear, right enough."

The assistant folded his arms and leaned on the counter. "I was telling the wife all about the fight last night and she said he'd been into her shop and didn't try anything on with her." He laughed. "She didn't know whether to be relieved or insulted."

Penny smiled. "And what shop does she work in?"

"The jeweler's. She remembered selling him something. Pair of earrings I think she said it was."

"Did they have a purple bead?" Penny asked.

The man made a wry face. "Ah, well now, you'd have to ask my wife that, wouldn't you?"

"Probably bought them for his wife," said Glyn. "Jewelry makes a good makeup gift, doesn't it?"

The assistant laughed. "I wouldn't know, thank God." As Glyn joined in the laughter, they turned their attention to the jingling doorbell just in time to see the door close behind Penny.

Penny's eyes swept up and down the counter, not seeing what she was looking for.

"Hello, may I help you?" A woman emerged from a small work area at the back of the shop.

"Oh, good morning. I'm here about a pair of earrings."

"Would you like us to make you a pair? Bogdan"—she tilted her head toward the man hunched over a workbench in the back—"does beautiful work."

"I know he does." Penny smiled. "He made me a beautiful snowflake brooch last year." Bogdan looked up from his bench, and recognizing Penny, he gave her a little wave.

"No, I want to ask you about a pair that I'm pretty sure were bought here. She reached into her bag for her notebook and, picking up a pen from the counter, quickly sketched the earring she had seen in the locked room at Ty Brith Hall, the mate to the one that had been found on Ashlee's body.

"It was shaped like this, and the stone here was purple. There was a little hook, silver, I think it was."

"I vaguely remember something like that but I think you should speak to Bogdan. If he made it, he'll know all about it."

She exchanged a few words with the jeweler, and he stood up, glanced at Penny, and then strode out into the shop. "Miss Brannigan. What may I do for you today? Another brooch, perhaps? Or has that policeman of yours got something else in mind?" He smiled at her.

"No, nothing like that, thanks." She hesitated, and then,

seeing her opportunity, began again. "Well, yes, actually, there is something I'd like. My policeman friend would have come himself, but he's very busy so he suggested I should speak to you myself.

"You see, I saw a pair of earrings on a woman in the supermarket. They looked like this." She pointed to the sketch on the counter. "They were so exquisite I thought perhaps you might have made them." The Polish jeweler beamed. "Yes, I did make them. Isn't that wonderful that you can recognize my work!"

"Yes"—Penny hurried on—"and now, you see, I would like a similar pair, if you don't think the lady who owns this pair would mind too much." The jeweler ran his hand over his chin. "I'd like mine in a different colour, of course," Penny continued. "Ah, red, we thought, yes, red."

"Of course," said the jeweler. "Red for St. Valentine's. How nice."

"And the lady you made this pair for, you don't think she'd mind?"

"Mrs. Bishop? No, I don't think she'll mind. I will make them slightly different. Won't be exactly the same. Do you like gold or silver?"

"Gold, I think, please. Now Mrs. Bishop—"

"Well, Mr. Bishop, he bought them. But when a gentleman buys jewelry, I learned a long time ago not to ask questions, and should I happen to see the gentleman at a social event or somewhere with his wife, I would never mention the jewelry. Especially if she was not wearing it."

"That sounds like a very smart policy," Penny said. "You just never know these days, do you?"

The jeweler laughed. "These or any other days."

236

"Now, Mrs. Bishop, is that the Mrs. Bishop who lives in Rosemary Lane, I wonder," Penny said innocently.

"No, actually, Penny, she lives just down the river from your Spa. Just a little farther down. The large house with the window overlooking the river."

"Oh! I know that house. I've often admired it from the tea shop across the river. How interesting." She picked up her notebook with the sketch of the earring in it and prepared to depart.

"You don't need to leave your phone number. I have it on file with my notes from the brooch."

"What? Oh, sorry, yes. For the earrings. Of course you do. Well, thank you."

Forty-one

Penny walked past the Spa and continued along the path that followed the River Conwy. A strong wind pushed at her back, once or twice almost causing her to stumble. But she kept on and in a few moments arrived at the Bishops' house. The glassed-in front of the building faced the river, but the entrance was at the rear of the house, a few metres from the path.

She knocked on the door and stood back. A few minutes later, the door was opened by a woman who appeared to be in her early thirties. She was thin, with shoulder-length blond hair. She wore jeans and a loose sweater. Her face was drawn and tired looking.

"Mrs. Bishop? I know you'll think this is very strange, and you don't know me, but I need to talk to you."

The woman frowned.

"Please. It's important."

"Who are you?"

"I'm Penny Brannigan. I need to talk to you."

"What about?"

"Before I say anything I need to know if your husband's at home. If he is, I'll leave. If he's not, please, may I come in? It's terribly important."

The woman hesitated. "He's out at the moment. What's all this about?"

"I've got a story to tell you. It's about an earring. And if it's true, which I think it is, you may be in great danger."

The woman stepped aside. "Come in."

She led Penny to a spacious, comfortable sitting room that overlooked the river, and gestured to a sofa covered in a yellow floral pattern with hummingbirds. The room was light and the sofa suited it.

From somewhere in the house Penny could hear the sound of the television playing. A children's program, she thought, judging by the music. Her eyes slid over to a photo on top of a small side table. A little girl with blond hair smiled out of a silver frame.

"Your daughter?" she asked. The woman nodded. "Please, just say what you've come to say, although I must say you look a little older than his usual type." She let out an unhappy little noise that might have been meant as a light laugh. "Oh, yes, I know all about them, if that's what you've come to tell me." She looked at Penny again. "Or perhaps you've come about your daughter."

"No," said Penny. "Not my daughter. But someone's daughter. A murdered daughter. A girl who left behind an earring that your husband had given her. I found it stuck in the floorboards of the room where she was killed. And I think she left it there to

240

tell us who killed her." The woman's hand had risen to cover her mouth. "Your husband. And I'm sorry to have to tell you this, but this young woman was pregnant and I think the DNA will prove that it was your husband's baby."

The woman's eyes closed for a moment. "But you knew that already, didn't you?" Penny said. "About the baby, I mean. Not about the other."

The woman shook her head slowly.

"I know this is a terrible shock to you, but can you think back to a time in early January when your husband behaved oddly? Was there a time when he should have been here and he wasn't? Or did he do laundry at an odd time? Late at night, maybe?"

"He missed our daughter's birthday," the woman said, almost to herself. "He promised to be here, but he wasn't. Wouldn't miss it for anything, he said, but then, of course, he did. Said he had to work. And he did do a laundry when he came in. I did think it odd at the time, but I forgot about it."

"You need to speak to the police right now," Penny said. "I can't tell you how urgent this is. If your husband thinks you suspect something, well, who knows what he might do? For your daughter's sake, you have to leave now. Where is she? Let's get her and we'll go."

But before the woman could respond, the distinctive sound of a key entering the lock in the front door, the tumblers falling into place, and the door opening froze the two women where they stood.

"Hey, babe, I'm home!"

Forty-two

*B*runo Bishop entered the sitting room, and after a quick glance at his wife, he fixed his eyes on Penny. "Who's this, then?" he asked.

"Have we met? I've seen you somewhere before."

"Bruno ah, this is . . ."

"I'm Penny Brannigan," Penny said brightly, digging in her handbag. "I'm the owner of the Llanelen Spa and I've come to let your wife know that she's the winner of our Valentine's Day spa day special. She's won a half day at the Spa, including a manicure and pedicure." She drew her lips up in what she hoped was something that would look like a sincere smile and not a frightened grimace and handed the man a business card.

"In fact, I was just about to suggest that we might head over there right now and get started." Penny picked up the woman's hand and looked at her fingernails. "Oh, dear me, it looks as if

I got here just in time. Well, we'll soon have those nails sorted out. Now then, where's your coat and we'll be off, shall we?"

"Now wait just a minute," said Bruno. "You're not going anywhere." He turned to his wife. "Who's going to look after Miranda?"

"Oh, didn't I say? She's coming with us. When we learned Mrs. Bishop had a daughter we made it a mother and daughter prize. We have the most adorable pink pearly polish that Miranda will just love." Penny cocked her head. "Where is she, by the way?"

"I'll get her." The woman exchanged a subtle glance with Penny and left the room. A moment later, the television music stopped and the woman reentered the room, leading a small girl by the hand.

"Hello, Miranda," Penny said. "I've come to take you and Mummy to the Spa for a manicure. Won't that be lovely?"

The girl looked up at her mother.

"What's a maniker, Mummy?"

"It means we're going to get our nails done, poppet. Penny has a lovely pink just right for you." The girl looked at her fingernails and frowned.

"Well," said Penny, edging toward the door and keeping up the smiling pretence, "nice to meet you, Bruno."

The two women, with the little girl between them, made their way into the hall. The woman took a small pink jacket off a hook and handed it to Penny, who helped Miranda into it. While she was doing this, the woman put on her own coat. With a glance back at the sitting room, where Bruno was standing staring at them with a puzzled look on his face, they turned to go.

"If anything happens," said Penny in a low voice, "you and

Miranda run for it. Go to the Spa and call the police. You'll be safe there." The woman nodded.

"Wait a minute." They turned toward the voice.

"You forgot this." Bruno held out the woman's handbag.

She took it from him, and they opened the door and stepped out into the crisp, cold air. With a quick glance at each other, they both grabbed one of Miranda's hands and, with her between them, walked down the river path. Neither looked back.

"Gonna get a maniker, Mummy."

"Yes, darling, you are."

Penny pulled open the door to the Spa, and with a glance over her shoulder, she stepped aside so the woman and her daughter could enter.

"Rhian," said Penny to the receptionist as she ushered the two ahead of her, "lock the door behind us and then ring 999. Ask for Bethan Morgan or Gareth Davies. Don't let anyone in except the police. Don't ask any questions. Just do it." Startled, Rhian rose from her seat and was obviously going to say something, but by then the trio had disappeared into the manicure room. Penny was just about to close the door when Mrs. Lloyd emerged from the hairdressing salon, her hair in curlers. "What's going on? Everything all right?"

"Everything's fine, Mrs. Lloyd. Please go back into the hair salon."

In the manicure room, a startled Eirlys turned around as Penny ushered in the woman and little girl. "Eirlys, this is . . .

oh, I've just realized, I'm so sorry, but I don't know your name."

"It's Emily," she said. "Emily Bishop." She gave a wan smile. "Yes, like the character on *Coronation Street*."

"What's going on?" asked Eirlys. "What is it?"

"Eirlys, I'm just going to step outside. You stay here with Emily, and why don't you show Miranda all the lovely nail polishes and she can choose a colour she likes. With Mum's approval, of course."

Penny stepped into the hall, closing the door behind her. She looked to her right, where an ashen-faced Rhian was standing beside her desk. At that moment Mrs. Lloyd emerged again from the hair salon, her hands folded beneath the animal-print haircutting cape fastened around her neck.

"Penny! There's something going on here, and I insist that you tell me what it is."

"I can't go into it right now, Mrs. Lloyd, but the police are on their way. Should be here any minute."

"Is the front door locked?"

"Yes."

"Oh, so we are in lockdown, are we?" She gave an excited little squeak. "I must call my niece, Morwyn."

"I'd rather you didn't, Mrs. Lloyd. We don't need a reporter here now. I really don't want you to do that."

"Oh, but you do, Penny, you do. You can't buy this kind of publicity."

"She's right. You can't."

Penny swung around to see Emily Bishop behind her. Before she could respond, there came a scream and then the sound of breaking glass. And then silence.

Forty-three

Bruno Bishop walked down the hall toward his wife, ignoring Rhian's shouts that the police were on their way. Mrs. Lloyd had scurried back into the hair salon and closed the door, leaving Penny and Emily Bishop staring down the hall at Bruno.

Why haven't the police arrived yet? Penny thought. I hope Mrs. Lloyd will know enough to ring them again and let them know the situation just got worse.

"What do you want?" she asked Bishop.

"I want my wife and daughter, and then we're getting out of here."

Emily took a step toward him. "We're not going anywhere and certainly not with a toe-rag like you. Now go back to the reception area and sit down and shut up. Leave us alone." She tipped her head in the direction of the manicure room door. "Miranda's in there and I don't want you upsetting her."

As she finished speaking, Sergeant Bethan Morgan and PC

Chris Jones entered the Spa, and as Rhian pointed the way, they walked down the hall. Penny's knees turned to jelly at the sight of them.

"Mr. Bishop, did you break that window?" Bethan got out her notebook.

"Yeah, I did," Bishop replied.

"Well, then, we'll be taking you down to the station, and we'd like you to come with us, Mrs. Bishop."

"What about my daughter?"

"We'll make sure she's cared for."

At that moment the door to the manicure salon opened and Miranda ran out, holding her hands in front of her.

"Daddy," she cried, "look at my maniker!"

As Bishop turned and lowered his head to examine his daughter's hands, Penny leaned into Bethan and whispered a few urgent words. She flicked a finger in the direction of his footwear and then straightened up.

"Oh, and Mr. Bishop," said Bethan, "we're going to be needing your boots. We'd like to run a few tests."

"Speaking of tests," said Penny, reaching into her coat pocket and handing her a small bag, "I expect you'll want to run a test on these, too."

She inclined her head in the direction of Bishop as Bethan opened the bag and peered at crumpled-up tissues, the blood on the tissues dried and brown.

Forty-four

"ello?"

"Oh, hi, Bethan." Penny listened for a few moments. "He did? I was right? But worse? Yes, please, come right over. About an hour? Okay, see you then."

Penny laid out a coffee tray and then switched on the television. But she was unable to focus, so she switched it off and picked up her laptop and checked her e-mail. She scrolled through a few messages, deleted a few, then closed the lid.

She checked her watch for the third time and sighed. And then, after what seemed like ages, came a knock on the door.

"Finally." She took Bethan's coat and led her into the sitting room.

"I've just made some coffee. Won't be a minute."

"I'll come with you."

Penny placed the coffeepot on the tray and carried it through to the sitting room.

"So tell me," Penny said when they were seated. "Tell me. What happened?"

"At first Bishop was cocky, very sure of himself, grinning, chewing gum, sitting comfortably." Bethan leaned back in the sofa and crossed her legs in a relaxed, casual posture. "But the DCI jumped right in. After the preliminaries were over—you know, we'd told him the room is wired for sound and video, everything is being recorded, you're not under arrest, you have the right to have a solicitor present—after all that and Bishop was all yeah, yeah . . . well then, DCI hit him with it. His first question caught Bishop off guard, and at that point I think he knew he was in big trouble."

"What did he ask?"

"He asked him the question you raised. Why didn't Bishop go to his daughter's birthday party?"

"And the reason he didn't go, of course, was because he was too busy killing and burying Ashlee."

"Right, but he didn't do it alone."

"No?"

"No. And this is where it goes really bad. He and the uncle, Tu', killed her."

"But why would Tu' kill his own niece?"

"Because"—Bethan took a deep breath—"because she was pregnant."

"Why would he care about that? Was it a family honour type of thing? I can see that Bishop would care—he was the father, wasn't he?" Bethan nodded.

"The DNA isn't done yet, but we expect it will show that he was, and even he's pretty sure that he was. He's not denying it."

"So I can see that Bishop wouldn't want his wife to find out, but why Uncle Tu'?"

"Because his sister, Mai, wanted out of the business. Once she'd got used to the idea, she rather liked the idea of becoming a grandmother. It changed everything for her. Now that she was going to be a grandmother, she didn't want any part of the business. But Tu' needed her because she was looking after the money laundering from the grow op. So when Ashlee was killed, he said, 'Well now that you're not going to be a grandmother anymore, you won't be backing out, will you?'

"It was quite chilling, really. And she was really conflicted, apparently. Her grief for her daughter and her loyalty to her brother."

She took a sip of coffee and picked up a biscuit.

"So this is what Bishop says, is it?"

"Yes, but Birmingham police will be re-interviewing Mai and Tu' based on this information."

"And Dilys?"

"He met her in the woods and tried to strangle her because she knew about the pregnancy, and then strung her up to make it look like she hanged herself."

"That's really gruesome."

"It's a lot to think about, isn't it?"

Penny nodded. "It is. And something that's been bothering me is why the drug gang would think this town a good place to set up a grow op."

"Ty Brith Hall was isolated and private enough that they felt secure. They had everything reinforced so no one could enter. If they'd had too much security, that might have got them noticed, so they tried to keep everything low key. People are often surprised that drug gangs would invest so much money in converting rental property, but the profits far outweigh the setup costs. The gang were also likely counting on the overly politically correct times we live in. If anyone had complained about them, they would have just cried racism. You wouldn't believe the things people get away with by playing the racism card."

She glanced at her watch, sighed, and stood up.

"Sorry, got to go. Hope all this won't keep you awake tonight."

"Oh, I'm sure it will."

Forty-five

The air was fresh, with an unexpected, earthy warmth as Penny and Trixxi walked up the road that led to Ty Brith Hall. In the cheerful manner of her Labrador breed, Trixxi bounded eagerly from one side of the road to the other, sniffing the familiar scents of what would always be her home.

As they reached the top of the road, just before it widened into the graveled area that led to the front door, a tall man with one hand raised came striding toward them. As he got closer, revealing dark hair, intense blue eyes, and a strong mouth set in a broad smile, Trixxi broke into a run. When she reached him, tail wagging hard, he bent down to stroke her and then stood up and offered his hand to Penny.

"Morning."

"Good morning, Emyr. You're looking well, all things considered."

He shrugged. "We'll get it all repaired. The damage was

extensive, but the structure itself is solid and it stood up well to the abuse—from the grow op and the police assault. It's mostly wiring and interior work."

They walked on together for a few steps, and then Emyr stopped and turned to Penny.

"Thanks so much for bringing her back. I realized it had been a mistake to leave her here but didn't know how to ask you if I could . . ."

"That's all right, Emyr, honestly. It was Gwennie who suggested that now you're back it might be a good idea for Trixxi to come home, too. But we were happy to look after her for you. She's a lovely dog."

"I'm hoping you'll let me give you something that might take her place," said Emyr. "After the fire we found a mother cat with her kitten huddled up in the back garden. The mother had been quite badly singed, but Jones the vet expects her to be okay. She'd probably been living in the stable and managed to escape with just the one kitten."

Penny winced.

"Would you like to see them?"

"Yes, I'd love to."

With Trixxi leading the way, they made their way around to the back of the house. Penny paused to admire the dolphin-shaped door knocker as Emyr opened the door. She stepped inside and walked down the kitchen corridor that had so recently been her means of escape.

In the kitchen, cuddled together in a towel-lined box in front of the Aga were a black-and-white cat and her kitten. The mother's paws were wrapped in bright pink bandaging and the fur on her ears was gone, revealing raw, blistered skin. "I have to put cream on them twice a day," Emyr said, bending over and scooping up her kitten.

He placed the kitten in Penny's arms. His milky blue eyes tried to focus on her face and he meowed softly. Penny rubbed his round, downy head with her chin. His fur was a soft dove grey and his tiny paws were white, as was a small, roughly heart-shaped patch on his chest.

"Oh, I don't want to put him down," Penny exclaimed, as the kitten nuzzled into her neck, his tiny, sharp claws catching on her jacket.

"Well, maybe you don't have to. I was wondering if you'd like to have him. I can't think of anyone who could give him a better home."

"I've never really thought about having a cat before, but maybe it's time I did get one." She smiled at him. "Thank you, Emyr, I'd love to have him." She gently detached his claws from her jacket and handed him back to Emyr.

"He's not quite ready to leave his mum, but when he is, I'll bring him round to you."

"And in the meantime, I can get in kitten supplies."

"I was just about to put the kettle on. Would you like a cup of coffee?"

"No, thanks. I had one already this morning."

"Well, thanks so much for bringing Trixxi back. May I offer you a ride home?"

"Thank you, Emyr, but no. If you don't mind, I'd like to walk down to have a look at the cottages and I'll make my way home from there."

"Sure, no problem."

"Have you had a chance to think about what you're going to do with the cottages? They're all empty now, aren't they?"

Emyr nodded. "I'll be applying for planning permission to do them up as holiday lets."

"Oh, that makes sense. There's wonderful walking around here and I'm sure you'll have no trouble renting them out."

Penny decided to ask the question that had been bothering everyone.

"Emyr, I hope you don't mind me asking, but at Christmas Gwennie said Ty Brith Hall had been sold, and it turned out the Vietnamese people were only renting it. What happened there?"

"Sure you won't change your mind about that coffee?" Emyr filled the kettle and gestured toward a chair.

"At Christmas it looked like the sale was safe, but my solicitor had concerns about the buyers' financing. He thought they were putting up too much cash and got suspicious. So we put in some conditions to try to stall the sale until the money could be investigated. On the solicitor's advice, I agreed the Vietnamese family could rent the property until we got the sale sorted. It's too big to just lie empty."

He shook his head. "I'm just so glad my father wasn't around to see the big mess I made of everything."

"You'll put it right," Penny said. "I think your dad would be proud of you. He'd know you did your best with the information you had."

He gave her a grateful smile.

"There's something else I wanted to talk to you about, Emyr, speaking of your dad." Penny told him about Dilys, who was recovering in hospital and had nowhere to go when she was discharged. "I know the cottage was given to Pawl to live in, but I wondered if you would consider letting her stay on in the cottage for a bit, if it's going to be empty for a while anyway. She might even be able to pay rent. Victoria and I are after the formula for her amazing hand cream, and of course we'll be paying her for it."

Emyr thought for a moment and then nodded. "I guess that would be all right. She can stay there for now, and maybe we can sort out something more permanent later."

After thanking him, Penny looked at her watch and then stood up.

"I must be off."

She gave Trixxi a good-bye pat and turned to go before Emyr could see her tears.

"Come and see us anytime. We'll be here. And thanks again for looking after her."

The sound of hammering grew louder as she approached the burned-out stable. The gaping hole, rimmed with black in the side of the building, had been covered with plastic sheeting. As she drew nearer, a workman waved her on. "Sorry, love," he said, "it's too dangerous. You can't come closer without protective gear." She waved in reply and continued on her way. The ground on each side of the path, still littered with dead brown leaves from the previous year, would soon be covered in a magical carpet of bluebells.

She passed the tree where Dilys had been found but could not bring herself to look at it.

She thought about Ashlee, so desperate to be loved, to belong. "It doesn't feel like home here," she had said.

But as Penny stopped for a moment to revel in the view of the snow-capped mountains, sometimes so cold and harsh and sometimes, as in this moment, magnificent as they shimmered in iridescent sunlight, this place felt like home to her.

This is where I belong, where my life is, and where the people I love are, she thought. She touched the delicate gold and red earring on her right ear. When Gareth had apologized for not getting her anything except flowers for Valentine's Day, she had laughed and told him that actually he had got her something else. When she told him about the earrings she had ordered at the local jeweler's, he had smiled and told her he was only too happy to give them to her.

"But let's call them a St. Dwynwen's gift," he had said, referring to Wales's patron saint of love and friendship.

She reached the end of the path and, inhaling sharply, slowly raised a hand to cover her mouth.

The end cottage, the one where Pawl and Dilys had lived, was transformed. The window box that a few weeks ago had seemed to be filled with nothing but dirt was now bursting with bright yellow daffodils, their trumpets waving gently in the light breeze. She remembered Dilys describing the box as all that remained of Pawl's gardening world. Acres of achingly beautiful gardens reduced over time to one window box on a grace and favour cottage. But as she stood there, appreciating the flowers in the window box as joyful, exuberant harbingers of spring, she was overcome by the meaningful splendor and brilliant simplicity of what Pawl had accomplished. He had done what he could and he'd done what he'd loved doing, just on a smaller scale, until the end. Most of us would wish that for ourselves and should be so lucky.

After one last, long look at the daffodils, drinking in their bright beauty and knowing the image and the memories would stay with her for a very long time, she raised her face to the warmth of the strengthening sun and turned toward home.